Libido Tsunami:

awash with the droll in life

Cate Burns

Savant Books and Publications
Honolulu, HI, USA
2016

Published in the USA by Savant Books and Publications
2630 Kapiolani Blvd #1601
Honolulu, HI 96826
http://www.savantbooksandpublications.com

Printed in the USA

Edited by Colleen O'Brien
Cover Art by Cate Burns
Cover Design by Daniel S. Janik

13-digit ISBN: 9780996325516

Dedication

I dedicate *Libido Tsunami* to the Four Sacred Directions, on the traditional Native American medicine wheel: North, South, East and West. Each symbolizes an archetypal and psychological state of the amazing but often befuddled human mind.

Acknowledgement

Thank you, Colleen O'Brien, for helping me see beyond, as you have valiantly done for the past thirty-five years.
I owe a debt of gratitude to Dr. Carl Jung (1875-1961), a Swiss psychologist who founded analytical psychology. As opposed to Sigmund Freud's focus on sexual energy (libido) as a main determinant of human behavior, Jung defined "libido" as an essential, but more generalized life-force energy that manifests in myriad forms of human vigor similar to Asian "chi" or Hindu "prana." In this book, I acknowledge and revere Jung's definition of "libido."

Table of Contents

Medicine Wheel West
A Flood of Family

On the traditional Native American medicine wheel, West is the place of emotion. With the many changes and losses we experience during a lifetime, we vent powerful feelings that, if we allow, can help us to transform ourselves.

A major source of the evocative and transformative takes place within my family; this is my theme in "Medicine Wheel West." Luckily, my family tradition is to laugh—a pleasant but devious way to frame, hide and disguise emotion. I dedicate the West to my large extended family.

Chapter 1
Six Elements of Light in Laughter

Light and joy are one; thus says every religious tradition. Like Eskimos with their many words for snow, my family has various kinds of laughter. Each could be likened to one of the types of light on a well-lit sphere: the Highlight, the Direct Light, the Half-Tone, the Cast Shadow, the Core Shadow and the Reflected Light.

In our family, the Highlight, the pinpoint of the brightest possible light of laughter is the wheeze. When something strikes us as hysterical, our mouths open wide (the fly-catching position) and we emit tiny, high-pitched scratching sounds (the ultimate state of mirth). A doctor would think we were suffering a deadly asthma attack. If you could see a photograph of me with my older cousin, Barb, who was my mom's age, you would see us gasping for breath, caught in a dreadful-looking paroxysm, reliving a memory of one of my mother's

3

fourteen fiancés: the Catholic one who gave her up for lent. Barb grew up with Mom and knew all her secrets, the source of infinite wheezes.

The Direct Light (bright, but not as intense as a Highlight) of laughter in our family is the belly laugh. When my family gets together, we tell competitive funny stories, each person trying to outdo the other. I thought everyone's family did this until I expressed this to an acquaintance, who gave me a completely blank, deadpan look. Regardless, we save up our best stories for family gatherings and hone our tales privately to individuals before we sit at the dinner table to let fly our best zingers. This year's prize goes to my sister, the fisherwoman, who insists to her grandkids that the way to deal with a fish is to land it, kiss it and return it to the lake. The next morning, as we gather at the beach, we see the grandkids seriously and quickly kiss the fish they catch. Sure enough, adult bellies shake all around, the children tentatively joining in once they catch sight of the general hilarity, a little confused about what could be so funny when they had acted according to instructions.

The Half-Tone is when laughter, like light, begins to dim in progression along the face of a shape, a place where shadow begins. I know the Half-Tone laughs well. We are a family of singers. No family gathering is complete without ukuleles strumming and favorite songs being bellowed. The Half-Tone songs are the ones that come toward the end of the evening. Did I mention that we are a family of heavy drinkers? This may be why we are singers in the first place and singers who become melancholy by the end of the day. When my dad would start the Whiffenpoof Song ("We are poor little lambs who have lost our way/Baa, baa, baa..."), he lent histrionic support to the loud "Baas" the kids belted out with great glee. But I would see a tear in his eye between the "Baas" ("Gentleman Songsters out on a spree/Doomed from here to eternity/God have mercy on such as we..."). You could say our family specialized in Half-Tone songs, since we were alcoholically primed for an increasingly depressed evening after the initial buzz wore off. Other family Half-Tone favorites were Auld Lang Syne, Ninety-Nine Bottles of Beer on the Wall, When Johnnie Comes Marching Home and Good Night, Irene.

Just because I am the only non-drinker in my family, do not think I am prejudiced against the types of light emitted by the drinkers. Last year, I attended a large Christmas Eve party hosted by my son's friend's family. I was reluctant to go because they were people I didn't know well. A typical family in Hawaii, they included every race, age, religion, size and shape—about fifty people in all. I expected the usual liquor bar, hilarity and family fights I was used to experiencing with my family at every holiday party throughout my childhood. Instead, the counter of beverages included only water, iced tea and lemonade. At the end of a somber evening, I commented to the host that I was startled to see no one drinking. He replied, as if surprised himself, "Oh, I guess we don't drink that much." Although I didn't say so to the host, I was also shocked there were no ukuleles, no Christmas carols, no dancing and not many jokes. Like a schizophrenic who refuses to take her meds because she craves the bizarre high energy, I love the elation of drinkers and, due to long years of childhood training, I put up with the dark side.

The Cast Shadow is the shade of a shape that is cast opposite and behind the light source. The Cast Shadow of jokes is dark humor, a family forte. Every summer we hold a large family reunion at the site of my (sadly, deceased) uncle's fishing cabin. This is acreage on a wide lush river where we camp, fish, swim, play baseball, kayak and inner tube down the river. We hold a midnight volleyball game in which balls that bounce off the giant Douglas firs count as safe. We build a super-sized bonfire (about ten feet in diameter) by the river and tell family stories. Even after decades of sitting at this fire, I hear new tales each year. Herds of elk wander nearby and unwittingly provide a lesson to those who overindulge. If someone passes out from drink, he is placed in a sleeping bag and gently carried near the bonfire for a little added warmth which he will need when the last stragglers leave the fire at three or four a.m. (an inbred chivalry, no doubt from our

British heritage, shines through the generations, for only men receive the rough elk treatment). The elk helpfully contribute their dung, which is shoveled into the sleeping bag and sealed with duct tape around the top. The morning antics of the unfortunate hungover cousin become one of the campfire stories, cruel, but very funny. And an effective deterrent to at least one or two future inebriants.

The Core Shadow is the darkest part of the shade; this is a familiar place for me to stand. My mother and I share ill fortune with men. One of her boyfriends kidnapped her, one preferred guys, and another had an unpleasant psychotic break. It must be genetic, for my history with male relationships is ditto. Mom had always created funny stories out of each disaster and I proceed to do the same, come what may.

When I found the teenaged love of my life necking with one of my best girlfriends in the back of a car, my immediate response was to tell them I was leaving for Africa. My broken heart only got me as far as Greece, but I still thought it was a great exit line that saved a little ragged dignity and allowed me to eventually limp back home and finish college.

Post college, I advanced to my next great amour who took a job in Europe. He bought a fancy motorcycle and together we planned to tour with me on the back. He was recently divorced (so he claimed) when I flew to meet him in Munich. Unfortunately, his not divorced wife met him there, too.

Someone floated the idea of attaching a sidecar to the bike to accommodate his new harem. No surprise, we all didn't get along well enough for the sidecar idea: round two of hobbling home from Europe ensued.

Worthy Core Shadows all. And, as time heals, the stories inch out of the Core Shadow dark and take on some humorous light.

Luckily, after the Core Shadow, there is one more kind of light: Reflected Light. It bounces off surrounding surfaces and illuminates the shadows. Reflected Light tends to glow rather than shine. And colors in Reflected Light are often deep and intense.

As I age in the Reflected Light of a greatly diminished personal belief in our society's Romantic Myth, I look around at my cousins who have experienced similar relationship problems—that pesky genetic factor again, no doubt. Although we believe nice men exist, experience has shown us that one appearing in our life is as likely as a reindeer flying. According to the Romantic Myth, a woman should become more sexy-looking when she needs to attract a man. In reality, I see that each of us has come to different resolutions. My cousins contently go gray-haired and saggy-skinned on nature's timetable. And, at the same time, one cousin, JoAnn, gathers animals around her: horses, dogs, cats, chickens, and any other stray that needs help. Another, Francine, simply relishes solitary quiet and intense happy relief of freedom from partnership problems. My cousin, Betsy, throws herself into building bigger sculptures. Jill works harder at her political committees. Nancy volunteers for six worthy causes at one time. And I absorb a little from each cousin as I eventually have come to chuckle at my past foibles while belting out songs in my Buddhist choir or sewing zany underwear or relishing time with my remarkable son. I continue to learn Reflected Light lessons from my family, as we are literally genetic reflections of one another.

There were one hundred and thirty people at our family reunion this year. As you might suspect, the lunch line gets long. My son patiently waited and slowly worked his way forward. Meanwhile, I had been reuniting with an older cousin, Billy, whom I rarely see. He shared his memories about my dad taking him on a fishing trip; they were sweet memories and precious to me because I have so few (Dad died when I was eight years old). "Hey," I said to Billy, "you have to see my son."

I hollered across the lawn, fifteen feet away, to Jon, first in line by now. I had to laugh at his woebegone look that seemed to beg, "Please, Mom, no more relatives right now. I just got to the front of the line."

I took pity. "Stay there, Jon, don't move. Just wave at cousin Billy, okay?" In his good-natured way, Jon smiled, waved and gave an apologetic look to Billy while we laughed. My cousin was a parent, too, and we were united in our sympathy for a hungry twenty-five-year-old in proximity to a feast. I watched his thoughtful look at Jon.

"It's amazing how much he looks like your dad—same height, same build, almost the same face." Billy's wondering eyes were filled with Reflected Light, just as mine are every time I look at my son.

Chapter 2
The Unconscious Bucket List

Having fought racial and gender prejudice throughout my life, imagine my surprise upon finding that in my sixty-fifth year, when I should have ramped up to argue against and correct age biases in our society, some inner part of me had already decided to accept old age gracefully. This sounds innocent enough.

When the idea of the "Bucket List" entered our culture about fifteen years ago, I dismissed it as hogwash. When our giant group of Baby Boomers began to age, they formed an agenda: they needed more stuff and more self-indulgence before they kicked the bucket, as if my generation hadn't commanded more possessions, drugs, sex and hedonism than any other in human history (Aside from Caligula, perhaps).

When I ask my friends if they have a Bucket List, they think for a moment and then respond, "Travel?" And then people will talk (and talk and talk and talk) about their commendable adventures around the globe. Travel used to be prestigious and exotic and, I suppose, to many folks it still is; it tops Bucket Lists.

I have no desire to travel to fulfill my ultimate wishes in this earthly realm. I view planes as cattle cars, giant germ factories transporting every local virus and bacteria to instant world dominion; in fact, airplanes and Bucket Lists seemed to be designed by a United Virus/Bacteria Network or UVBN, as in, You've Been Had. I'm really not the pessimist my ex-boyfriend thinks I am. As I told him over and over throughout our many happy years, I'm just a realist. In fact, germ laboratory air travel is a good thing; like smallpox, this modern plague will cull out inferior genes, leaving the superior specimens to strengthen our species.

But this begs the larger question. I wonder about my generation's need for more accomplishments before they die. Is that really what life is about? Is there such a thing as being ready to die? If I have jumped out of an airplane (another item high on Bucket Lists), will I be more ready to die than if I had not done so? I can't imagine drawing my last breath and sighing, "I'm so glad I went skydiving."

I work for hospice and I recognize that people can die with a wholesome conscience if they have "cleared the decks:" made a will, told their family "I love you" (if they do), confessed or otherwise resolved negativities to a trusted counselor or minister about lingering issues that could create conflict in their last moments, cleaned the closets (literally and/or figuratively) and basically done whatever can create a peaceful mind.

If I don't want to travel and I have already completed the practical pre-death tasks, a Bucket List is a moot point. Therefore, I decide to be a non-conformist and to reject the Bucket List as a silly Baby Boomer fad. So I am not prepared when it sneaks up and bites my sub-conscious on its rear end.

As I approach my sixth or seventh decade, I can't help but wonder if a certain activity might possibly provide the finishing touch to that task. For example, during recent dental work, I joked with my dentist, "Will this last me out?" And I was sincerely glad when he assured me it would. Not just glad: Inside, I felt a resonate "Whew," a sense of resolution, relief that I had done something good and final. I was surprised at what a positive feeling this was.

A few months ago, I became aware of an unexamined list of "Somedays" I harbor. My financial advisor told me I had a little wiggle room in my budget, and up popped the "Someday, if I Could Ever Afford It" list. My friend is a weaver of sublime tapestries, and my budget inched into the stratosphere (for me): enough to buy two. I snagged them up and feel daily delight living with them. Fortunately, the Someday List completed

13

itself with these joys.

I also notice a desire to make life easier on my son. Besides a will, I don't want to leave him a big physical mess to clean up when I die. Hence, I began to downsize, forcing myself to throw away about half my belongings, an effort that has taken several years. I recently had reason to appreciate our family pet, a cockatiel, a jolly fellow who helped my son through adolescence. After talking to a friend with horses and another friend with dogs, I have new appreciation for our bird, James. When a beloved horse dies, my horse-loving friend has multiple large boxes of ashes filling her barn. When my other friend's dog dies, she is left with a shoebox of ashes on her mantle. When a neighbor's cockatiel died, she lamented she had only a teaspoon of ashes. But now I know I chose the right pet for my vigorous downsizing efforts; his future jigger-sized funeral "urn" will have a place of honor on my small night-table next to my bed. (Although, at the moment James sits on my shoulder chirping, "Stop writing about my death.")

My beloved and rather stubborn son (Where did he get that trait?) held out for months for the perfect job. I secretly began to worry he might never find that job and become a drifter through life; I began to try to make that okay by telling myself, "Ambition only leads to heart attacks. Isn't it nice he is such a relaxed person who enjoys computer games so much?" It didn't work, though finally, at age twenty-six, he found a good job.

But I am astounded at my inner reaction; a huge piece of me had been afraid he could not survive in the cold world. Witnessing proof of his capabilities, I feel a great release. I could let go and die happily because my son would be okay in the real world.

As I age, cycle completion has reared its head, as in, I was never good at X. But, I want to prove to myself competent in X before I die, or gracefully accept that I am a total loser at X and be done with it; which reminds me of Mrs. Bishop, my college freshman English teacher. At that time, I saw myself as an English major, a budding writer of renown. But I rarely understood one word Mrs. Bishop said in English 101 and I couldn't achieve above a "C" in her class. Heartbroken, I concluded I was a lousy writer and diverted to another career. But I never stopped writing and savoring literature throughout my life; I have allowed myself to enjoy it deeply regardless.

Besides making life easier for kids, cleaning up old ineptitudes and adding little joys to daily living, a couple of specific and unexpected "Do This and You Can Die Happy" events recently shocked me with their intensity. One day it occurred to me, if I died tomorrow, my ex-boyfriend would have been the last person I had ever had sex with in my entire life; a very depressing realization. Fortunately, I was able to correct this situation in the most delightful way. But, of course, once I finished my relationship with Mr. Delight (and with a less troubled breakup than most), the original question remained. Could I accept that he might be the last one? I could see this type of Bucket List had become a hamster wheel and decided not to pursue it any further.

I finally saw that certain types of Bucket Lists had raised their hairy and rumpled heads in my life: Will X Last Me Out Until the End List, Someday if I Could Afford It List, How Can I Leave Less of a Mess for My Son List, Will My Son Be Okay in the Real World Checklist, Last Ways I Want to Prove Myself Competent List.

My nephew is in his early forties and his enlightened workplace encouraged him to do a Bucket List project. Did he focus on indulgent travel or leaps from airplanes? No. In a saintly gesture, he transcribed my grandfather's long British Navy journal written in the 1870s and '80s aboard Her Majesty's ships all over the world. Grandfather's writing was vertical and formal, but he was apparently unaware that punctuation had been invented, so the journal was a two-hundred-plus page sentence. My nephew's Bucket List transcription of the journal is a grand gift for our whole extended family. If this is what the next generations does with their end-of-life anxiety, I am all aboard.

I am now a convert to the Bucket List; however, mine is an unconscious, fluid process of surprise and synchronicity. It is natural to face end-of-life issues in one's last decades. And I don't blame my generation for trying to take control of the process and force it to be travel or skydiving. But I commit to riding the rollercoaster of life, facing its amazements, insights and opportunities until the end without losing the serendipity, and sometimes seeming craziness of it all.

Chapter 3
Curious Comfort

Stuck in a kayak with Maile, an old childhood friend, I paddled until my arms burned. She had wanted me to sit in the back to steer and provide most of the muscle. I caved in and faced a powerful headwind, fiercely paddling, gaining little. With Maile, frustration was the norm. When provoked, she could come out with fists flailing. I was a little afraid of her. But, afflicted by stubborn optimism, I hoped for the best. Maybe today she wouldn't berate me for steering the kayak off course or criticize my love of blue jeans, which she hated. Why did I prolong the thirty year connection that, by all rights, could have easily ended when I moved out of the neighborhood years ago? My track record with difficult relationships prevailed; I naively hoped to conquer my fear of her and build a deeper friendship.

The sun was bright off the Waianae coast of Oahu. I savored the turquoise waters while I labored, until Maile pointed ahead and yelled, "Dolphins!" I saw small brown blobs in the distance, not jumping and spinning as I thought they should, but swelling out of the water just enough to breathe. I redoubled my battle with the headwinds, focusing on my arms that would surely soon look as beautiful as Michelle Obama's.

This was my first experience kayaking near dolphins and I learned they were fast swimmers. I feared Maile's distain, or even wrath, as I paddled like a mad woman, thinking I'd never catch up with them. But Maile gleefully pointed and called, "Over there, over there." I ignored my aching arms and powered on. Striving against all odds was a favorite pastime of mine; just ask my daily inebriated mother or my philandering ex-boyfriends.

All at once, a group of five or six dolphins surfaced next to us. At last, they were here. I expected a Flipper moment: a dolphin would stop and look me in the eye with a telepathic healing message. Miraculously, my life would change and I would no longer date drunks or succumb to the back seat of a kayak. But the dolphins rushed by with shiny brown backs. Not one face did I see. However, I heard their strong inhalations, taken in unison, a chorus of breath that caused me to inhale with them.

I glanced behind me—more dolphins. On all sides, dolphins.

20

"Look, Maile, look." I had heard dolphins would swim in a large circle to corral fish for lunch. I chuckled and relaxed my arms. Were we the prey?

In a flash, they left. A moment later, I saw them swimming in the distance. Once more, I vigorously paddled, aiming for them. For the next hour, the pattern repeated several times, a dolphin game. I dug in the water to catch up with the large pod only to be unexpectedly surrounded. Maile and I laughed like children. Then, they zipped away and we worked to find them once more. At last, they rushed to the far horizon and I laid the paddle across my seat, feeling replete, as if I had eaten a delicious Thanksgiving dinner that I had prepared all by myself.

Incredibly, without a single dip of the paddle, the wind blew us neatly to our dock. Back at our bed and breakfast, Maile and I had a cup of tea on the spacious lanai. Relaxed, we gazed at the bay we had been in an hour before. I felt a new quiet with her, the kind you share with your easiest family members.

But I couldn't find words to describe this strange comfort until Maile said, "You know, Cate, all these years, I felt like there was a barrier between us. But, it's odd; now that we don't live nearby, I feel closer to you."

"You're right, Maile," I said. "I felt the wall, too. Now I'm really glad we kept our friendship going."

And I was, except when I thought of Maile's temper, part of

21

her character like a rumbling, sometimes spurting volcano. But somehow, I didn't feel fear or dread it anymore when I imagined her explosions; I knew they weren't aimed at me. Maile was a primal force of nature. Now I could accept a potential eruption from her more objectively, and felt free to appreciate her crisp honesty.

I took a long sip of tea, happy that I had tried one more time.

Chapter 4
TWNBD or Twin Bed

Since childhood, it has been my educational (accidental or perhaps karmic) privilege to live around people who are skilled at finding such a spectacular niche in their lives that they inspire reverence and awe in all those around them, myself included. They seem to achieve every ego's fantasy: to be an ultimate authority, a role doctors enjoyed several decades ago.

In America, we can't rely on differing accents to define our status as the British have traditionally. In our relative classlessness, it takes cleverness to figure out how to inspire worship. Having lived in the shadow of revered personages, I early learned it was beyond me to aspire to their heights. My father and mother both had this talent (that they did not pass on to their offspring). Handsome, beautiful and alluring, they were the king and queen of the neighborhood. Dad was a Secret Service agent for Presidents Roosevelt, Truman, Eisenhower and Vice-President Nixon. In those pre-Watergate days, Dad warned us never to trust him if we found ourselves at a poker table with the VP. As he routinely carried a load weapon and had a feisty temper; no one dared cross him.

After Dad's early death (his heart failed him, not a gun), Mom became a Special Education teacher and combined this erstwhile virtue with her blond bombshell charisma to give her a larger than life persona. Party central, our home had an open-door policy where anyone could come at any time of the day or night. Recently, an old family friend reminisced, "I never knew what would happen when I stopped by to visit your mom, but I knew it would be hysterically funny and a great time." This was said after he waxed nostalgic about the bottle of his favorite whisky she would plant next to him upon his arrival. I nodded and smiled and didn't say much in response, not wanting to shatter any illusions. Let him have his good memories.

Having lived so close to such exalted souls, I saw their very human shortcomings: for example, Dad's non-stop beer swilling (a chilling fact in proximity to his guns) and Mom's daily post-5 p.m. coffee mugs (at least two) of straight vodka, one ice cube per mug. Alcohol fueled their sparkle, but no one around them seemed to notice or judge at the time. And I had to grow up before I made these connections. However, I have never lost admiration for my parents. They pulled off one of the biggest coups humans can achieve: how to become gods.

Trained since earliest memory to be a celebrant at their

24

altars, I have naturally carried this trait into adulthood, attracting god-like people, mostly men, who need acolytes to support them. Humans worshipped as gods would seem Egyptian or Medieval, and as such hopelessly out of fashion in the modern age. But I have learned the desires to be adulated and, in turn, to venerate others, the two fitting together like the Yin-Yang symbol, representing eternal human traits. Although I grew up to be strong, independent and self-supporting in the feminist age, a sneaky underground part of me leads me inexorably to bond with Those Who Need to Be Deified— TWNBD or Twin Bed.

Yes, one might correctly predict that all my boyfriends were Twin Beds. My skill at locating these types astounded me and each time I promised myself, "Never again." But I was repeatedly fooled by variations on the theme.

Mother demanded high educational standards of her children and also revered artists as the "greatest humanitarians." I cleverly combined her values in my first serious boyfriend, an art professor, Ed. Mom and Ed adored each other. After several years, when I left Ed (he had beaten me after imbibing, no surprise, a bottle of whiskey), she deeply mourned and predicted I would never achieve such high social status again in my life. Too mortified to tell her the truth about Ed, I said she was free to see him as much as she wanted.

I outdid Ed in my next boyfriend. To all appearances a quiet and humble man the opposite of Mom, Dad and Ed, he was the sweetest, most generous, thoughtful and intelligent man I had ever met. Upon entering a room, Vince immediately made sure everyone had a comfortable chair, was warm enough, and had a glass of water (he did not drink alcohol, glory hallelujah). If one of these conditions was lacking, he busied himself fetching the needed object or building up the fire. I was a fool for kindness, and this is how he effectively wooed me. Compared to my family of boisterous impulsives, Vince seemed a cut above, in a caste beyond anything I had ever dreamed of. I placed him high on a pedestal. Vince must have sensed that initial impressions tended to last. I was like a baby bird imprinted with, "Vince is the nicest guy on earth and always will be forever."

It took me years to understand his other tactics. In a group, he subtly made sure everyone knew he had sold his computer company for one-half million dollars; this would be indicated in some vague, innocent reference that was far outshone by his modesty and self-deprecating sense of humor. As one of my outspoken girlfriends said, "I just love Vince. He is the most humble almost-millionaire I ever met." Just what he wanted everyone to think. An artist in his own way, Vince mixed some money with a lot of humility in the correct proportions to create an unbeatable persuasive appearance: Mr. (Wealthy) Sweet and Innocent Nice Guy. In the early years, I admit my ego was cravenly swayed by his pristine façade. How could I ever have suspected hidden deviousness?

I never thought to question why he needed to show such a squeaky clean image to the world. It took me years to discover what might have become obvious to most readers by now: he hid a high-risk secret life which no one would believe unless one had seen direct evidence, which I eventually did.

Post Vince, I became determined, once again, never to place another human in the stratosphere above me. No more Twin Beds! When I looked back, I could see that, no matter how determined I had been to choose more wisely after Ed, in reality, Vince proved a more extreme case. I was regressing. With this depressing reality, I took a ten-year break from men. I read every book I could about personalities who feel superior and the enablers (me) around them. I learned there are certain Red Flags I could look for in this type of difficult personality. And sure enough, I can now spot them before I want to marry them.

My studies taught me that narcissists and others who feel superior gravitate toward professions that give them maximum respect and credibility, which I call Unassailable Positions— top techie nerd, psychiatrist, New Age pundit, hospice chaplain, Board Member (corporate, academic or charitable) or any other niche within an organization that gives them a power monopoly with a "great guy/gal" mystique (think Bernie Madoff). Society assumes these people are beyond reproach, modern saints (until they fall). On the National Public Radio humorous news quiz show, "Wait, Wait, Don't Tell Me," a contestant calls in live, on air during the show, and states his name, location and profession. Recently, when a man stated his profession to be "hospice chaplain," the audience clapped and cheered, something I had never heard happen in my ten years of listening to the show. Furthermore, the host made a remark about everyone else's jobs being meaningless compared to this gentleman. The chaplain sounded like a very nice guy, but, so was Vince.

I love to study healing methods from indigenous cultures, but it is a constant exercise for me to keep these highly esteemed women and men off my reverence pedestal. Even though the New Agers around may not hesitate to believe that one can heal at a distance or reads auras, I keep my feet on the ground. No more Twin Beds.

I meet the same challenges with the highly respected Tibetan lamas with whom I study Buddhism. While these men have realized well-documented achievements that stagger the western mind, they are very down-to-earth, and this helps me keep them there.

Most of those in Unassailable Positions do not harbor a nasty double life. But, the cynic in me still quakes if I meet someone in a revered position and s/he pops out a Red Flag. I want to shout, "Look out" to all those around me. I volunteer for a hospice non-profit and one day, when I met the chaplain (now no longer employed there) for the first time, I was surrounded by a group of volunteers. Within one minute he locked the group with a prolonged unblinking stare, in a successful effort to control, manipulate and insult us. Typical Red Flag. I did not marry him. But I was astounded to see how tolerant everyone else in the group was; no one showed the least impatience or judgment, as if it was his right (as a saint) to keep us two hours late and scold us and our boss for his list of bad things we would no doubt do in the future. In fact, over the years, I was astounded to see this chaplain universally revered. Luckily I could do my work while keeping him right where I wanted him: far away from me.

Aside from memorizing Red Flags, I try to consciously control my need to raise someone I respect up into an exalted sphere while I lower myself at the same time as if in the grip of immeasurable gravitational forces. To help counter these destructive powers, I became a religious person and joined a temple in order to keep my desire for reverence in an appropriate heavenly realm and out of the human.

If I ever again make my bed and sleep in it with a partner, perhaps there is a smaller chance it will be a Twin Bed.

Chapter 5
I Will Never Leave You

When I visited my son, Jon, in Denver, he wanted to share his passion for skiing with me, but, at sixty-five years old, I had unconsciously assumed a prejudice about my age that immediately roared into my consciousness: "You will break all your old bones and they'll never heal," it said with a menacing grin. Never one to resist my son for long, I timidly agreed on a trip up a mountain, perhaps to ski.

When Jon was born, I had lived in a ski town at Lake Tahoe for more than fifteen years and coveted the silent cross country skiing trails. But my son wanted to teach me downhill where other skiers shot by me like bullets, rendering me a jittery mass of nerves. Jon's dad had been skiing with Jon since Jon had moved to Denver (skiing was something we rarely had time for at Lake Tahoe), and I embarrassed myself with twinges of jealousy. I had to prove I was as good a parent as Jon's dad.

As we left Denver, Jon excitedly proclaimed a forecast of 28 degrees, a perfect temperature to keep the powder from melting. I foresaw instant death from hypothermia at 12,000 feet.

As we drove uphill, the weather news became worse, forecasting a snowstorm, and, indeed, as we headed up the mountain, clouds of snow began hitting our windshield.

"This is great! Fresh powder all day with this storm," Jon exclaimed.

"Uh, umm," I said. I hated to look like a wimp to my son. "Well, I have to tell you the truth. I don't know if I can ski in a snowstorm, Jon. Before you were born, we had a bunch of skiers come visit us at Lake Tahoe and we went to ski at Heavenly in a big squall. The flakes were huge, not tiny like these." I pointed out the window. "And they were thick and blowing at me; it was a white-out sometimes. Everyone else was a good skier and they all took off and left me somewhere at the top of the mountain all alone. I was lost and a beginner skier. I could barely do the snowplow. I was terrified."

"Oh, Mom, I would never leave you," Jon said with intensity. As usual, he had honed in on the crucial part of my story.

I felt my eyes heat up with tears. All my life, I had wanted someone (mother, father, boyfriends) to simply stay with me. None of them had. I felt Jon's promise deep in my center of gravity; he would be with me on the peak, come what may.

Jon and I arrived at our snowy mountain and geared up. As we rode the gondola, I said a fervent prayer that it would break down so I could dangle for an hour enjoying the spectacular white and shadowy mountains. At the 12,000-foot bunny hill, I was surprised to discover I didn't immediately die in the frigid air. Jon was right; I was warm and the small Rocky Mountain snowflakes fell like fairy dust providing perfect powder with ample visibility.

I remembered more about skiing than I thought. Jon proved an astoundingly patient teacher, staying with me the whole day to review the basics, bit by bit. I had never seen that side of him before.

After several more trips to this mountain over the next year, with Jon's easygoing perseverance hour after hour, I attempted the pinnacle (for me) of skiing achievements: the hockey stop. The goal was to keep my skis parallel and turn them abruptly forty-five degrees to stop myself on any slope. Like a child learning to walk, I pushed myself into motion, gained speed, then threw my body into the task, in my case, an uphill twist while digging in my heels, and, at the same time, lifting and rotating the uphill ski. Resembling a toddler, I often forgot one crucial element. Over and over, at least a dozen times per run, I tried to control my jerky and unruly muscles. My son hovered, calling out encouragement, compliments and suggestions. It must have been very boring for him, except that I was his mother and he probably did not want to pick up the pieces, should I crash. When I finally put all three elements together into a semblance of a hockey stop, enormous joy welled up inside my chest.

"Hey, Mom, you're looking good. You're really doing it," my son called.

The hockey stop: sign of being a real skier, not a wannabe. Even with all my years on the cross country trails, I hadn't realized that I never felt like the genuine item. Jon said I needed three or four more ski trips to perfect the hockey stop, to feel it in my bones (all intact, by the way). But I already felt pride in my accomplishment and deep delight in my enhanced relationship with Jon.

Later in the day, Jon declared I was ready for a green run. We didn't realize that it was past 4 p.m., a time that changed our sport into what the resort called "night skiing." In the softening dusk, the crowds disappeared and we were often the only ones to be seen on the slope. The petite snowflakes glistened with the last rays of sun. I relaxed into the hill and let it carry me. The long shadows gently consumed me as the whole mountain became magic. With my son's ever-close protective presence, I fell in love with skiing.

But the green run was supposed to end at a chair lift about one quarter of the way down the mountain. It didn't. Large orange barriers blocked our route to the lift. Jon and I had both known I could comfortably make it to this spot where I could ride the rest of the way down. We had no choice but to continue, hoping for another chair lift soon. Down and down we went, and my muscles began to wobble with fatigue. I couldn't get enough breath in the thin air to supply my muscles. With rubbery thighs, I stopped to rest every fifteen vertical feet. I hated making my son wait for me. Each inhaled spasm felt as though it went all the way through me, but it never provided enough air. At last we realized that, with night skiing, all the chair lifts closed except the one at the bottom and the one at the top. I would have to ski all the way down.

No matter how much I rested, my leg muscles finally rebelled and stopped moving. I slowly sat in the snow, Jon suspended above me, worried. As I tried to catch my breath, my stomach flopped over with nausea. Altitude sickness. Typical of me, I waited to tell Jon how badly I felt until I was sure death loomed. "I'm going to hurl," I moaned to my son.

The mountain gods were with us. Ski patrol appeared up ahead on a snowmobile. Jon zoomed up to him and explained our situation. "Sure," the rotund young man on the long black vehicle said. "Climb aboard. I can go through all the barriers. I'll take you over to the gondola. It's quite a way from here and up a hill." He eyed me, bent over with heaving breaths. "I don't think you'd make it without a ride." Swallowing my pride and trying to keep my stomach calm, I tottered to my savior. There was only room for two on the snowmobile and I knew Jon wanted to speed off on his own anyway.

"See you at the bottom," I warbled between breaths.

"I'll meet you there," Jon said. And he was there long before I glided down on the gondola, my legs, breath and stomach relishing quiet gulps of air that nourished me as quickly as a candy bar. When I saw Jon waiting for me, offering to carry my skis (even my arm muscles shook), I felt a wave of joy, relief and love. That, and a hot meal with a long night's sleep got me back up on the slopes the next day.

True to his word, Jon took great care of me on that mountain, no matter what.

Chapter 6
Dionysus

I came from a very religious family; my parents worshipped Dionysus, the Greek god of drink. An ancient, but robust religion, it featured a lovingly maintained shrine packed with cut crystal pieces filled with sparkling rainbow-colored liquids.

As with most religions, dissent was not permitted, not even recognized to exist. Everyone over the age of eighteen who entered our door had to drink, no exceptions. And to those under eighteen, a blind eye graciously extended. Everyone in our neighborhood and larger family lauded this as the superior way to live. My parents were acclaimed atop a pantheon of supreme beings (all fellow drinkers). Today, fifteen years after my mother's death and fifty years after my father passed, neighbors still lament that they did not spend more time with them to absorb their great wisdom: they were the handsomest, the smartest, and the sexiest, like neighborhood deities.

Within the family, we all followed the sacred rules of our cult. No locked doors allowed; anyone walked in our home at any time of the day or night to, as Mom loudly proclaimed, "drink, smoke and fornicate as much as they wanted." We were party central and proud of it. When celebrants came in our door, mother immediately ushered them to the shrine; the priestess presided over the sacraments and knew the best libation for each individual. If she wasn't home, my brothers and I became the hosts and offered the nectar of Dionysus to our guests.

No criticism of any drunken brawl passed our lips; indeed the ritual madness of the cocktail "hour" (5 p.m. to pass-out time or bedtime) became codified as sublime events. The most extreme examples inspired Mom's stories, repeated for years. Aside from the liquor, the recurrent litanies formed a religious service of sorts, complete with sermon, for her sycophants. Mom lived to entertain an audience. When I grew up in Seattle, the fanciest restaurant was called Canlis. Mom referred to it as a kind of heaven in statements such as, "When I win the lottery, the first place I will go is Canlis." Years after my father passed away, one of Mom's dates finally asked to take her to the revered restaurant overlooking Lake Union. Days before, she touted her new status as a prospective visitor to the gods' realm. The day after the sublime visitation, she had a new story she re-told with glee for decades. The short version: She had so many pre-dinner cocktails, by the time her expensive dinner came, she threw up on it, filling the plate to overflowing. Apparently she still had memory function, for she praised the suave waiter who swished a cloth napkin over her meal and whisked the offense out of sight. She was the female Dionysus thumbing her nose at the Olympian dominions, ever rejoicing in her liberated behavior that knew no bounds.

As a child growing up in that home, I was taught to venerate freewheeling antics such as the Canlis saga. When I was nine years old, an old family friend, a man Mom's age, chased me around the house waving a whale's penis bone at me while the adults and teenaged boys shouted obscenities, I learned to laugh even when filled with terror. When Mom belted out her favorite song, Frankie and Johnnie, about a woman (Frankie) who shot her lover dead (Johnnie), that she only sang in a black-out state as she barely stood in front of her audience, stumbling and shooting with her index finger, I learned this was funny. At any age from 6 to 19, when drunken adult men pulled me into dark corners to kiss me, I learned they were unsteady and easy to escape. During all of these supposedly hysterical epic occurrences, I laughed. But inside, I wondered why humor made my stomach twist like the lemon peel in Mom's drinks. What piece of the puzzle did I miss? Obviously the ninny, I didn't understand what everyone else found comic.

I grew up feeling like I missed the party; I mistook the

meaning of life. Many times, I wanted to ask Mom, "Why is Frankie and Johnnie funny?" when it's clearly sad. Why split your sides over a scientific specimen from a whale? Why chase me, a little kid? Why was hurling on a Canlis dinner comical? I felt sorry for the waiter and embarrassed for my mother. And why would slobbery old men secretly kiss a child? All sacrilegious questions I instinctively did not ask. But Mom must have caught me with a quizzical look or not laughing hard enough because, thousands of times, she told me there was something wrong with me and that I never understood her sense of humor. But as a child, I badly wanted to love the party and be a starlet next to Mom.

My mother had the loudest voice in our family, and while she admitted that certain neighbors might not agree with her, she would point out that they attended church on Sundays and that fact automatically negated any credibility they might have had. The divine energies contained in her bottles were the only source of the sacred that existed.

In my twenties, I finally realized that the firm rules concerning alcohol in our household comprised a religious order and that the Greeks had already invented it. To Mom, the ecstasies of her daily revelries were personal; after all, in the Greek pantheon, Dionysus was the only god who actually entered you through celestial libations, so that you became the god. Sure enough, my drunken mom existed on a plane above the human realm. She sang and danced with wide gestures as if on a stage surrounded by dozens of adoring acolytes.

I never dared suggest to her that her rules and prejudices were as strict as an evangelical creed, for she did not like to have her pedestal shaken. I did my utmost to stay on Mom's safe side, even trying to share her love of drinking with her. But oddly, given my background, no alcohol tasted good to me. And if I consumed a half-cup or more of even the milder beers or wines, my stomach quickly rebelled. My twenty-fifth birthday present to myself was to stop trying to drink.

Age brought further insight. As an adult, I understood that a whale penis would appear hilarious to an inebriant; and that drunks were mean and would chase a young girl around waving the giant appendage as a joke. Eventually, I learned that drink and promiscuity went together and were easily aimed at the young and defenseless. And I comprehended Mom's avant-garde barf at Canlis similar in intent to the alcoholic artist Jackson Pollock pissing in Peggy Guggenheim's fireplace in front of her and her friends to express his anti-elitist disdain. I still didn't see anything amusing about Frankie and Johnnie.

After twenty-five years of toadying up to Mom, trying to love her non-stop parties but never fitting in, one bright day, I discovered the true me: I hated Mom's drunkenness. I continued to love Mom, but not while she was imbibing, about half the day. Glory be, I accepted myself as an outcast to one-half of her life and to ninety-six percent of her as a Dionysus devotee, a vision which persisted in her psyche throughout her sober hours. This left little of her that I could relate to, adult daughter to mother from the hours of 9 a.m. to 10 a.m. while she drank her morning coffee and pretended she wasn't hung over before weekend visitors arrived for the day's bash. I decided to venerate reality, however brief a period it was, more than liquor's illusions.

With this new honesty, I took Mom off her goddess throne. My party criteria for choosing friends (till now, the flashiest) no longer sufficed, and I searched for better ways to choose companions. I found myself with an odd win-win emotional advantage derived from the outsider perspective I had unwillingly acquired. At the low end of the totem pole already, I had nothing to lose in personal relationships and hence learned the art of seeing bad behavior in others, rating it and dumping the worst. Boyfriends were the best ones to practice on. With her fourteen fiancés, infinite dates and three husbands, Mom created a handy template for me: she taught me that flushing most men out of one's life was a woman's job and she was the expert. Being my mother's daughter, I had already achieved my lifetime quota of rude behavior from others; with this tank-topped off, I was ready to test my new, higher set of social intentions on a random assortment of new boyfriends.

At first, of course, each man I met was the nicest guy I could

42

imagine. But when I discovered Rev. Jack didn't own a car and expected me to research and choose restaurants along his bus route, I said, "No thank you." When, on the second date, Rick and later Ben's hands began roaming, out they went. Bennett was a whiner. Floating with Pat in his home-made hot tub, he sobbed non-stop about the ex-girlfriend he had broken up with three years prior. In spite of the surprisingly efficient hose he had rigged up explicitly for female pleasure, I did not return. Chris #1 stalked me long after I told him to leave and Chris #2 rear-ended my car "by accident." Being kind to Phil, I at first paid for half of our dates and later, more than half. After a few months, he asked me to finance his chukar hunting trip to rural Nevada and he would give me half the chukars. I offered him a one-way ticket to Elko. Joe spent more time with his ex-girlfriend "helping her" than with me. I'm sure my dating history is no different from most women's. But I learned from the worst and can now happily reject the jerks, and thank every single one for allowing me to flex my discernment muscles.

There is nothing so liberating as discarding an imposed religion and feeling fully free of its strictures. I rejected bacchanalia beliefs like I tossed out the bad-apple men. I chose to avoid bars and not to drink alcohol. I now keep locked doors 24/7 and don't give out my address (sorry, Mom—you dearly wanted a carbon copy daughter, and fate dealt you a cruel blow with me). I enjoy drinkers for a while, but when I stop enjoying them, I move to another room. If anyone asks, I no longer sugar-coat; I'm willing to describe the offensive behavior in detail. Interestingly, I find few drinkers today defend obnoxious inebriation with Mom's gutsy superiority. Nowadays, people tend to make psychological excuses for the drunk, such as, "She puked on you because she had such a hard day/week/month/year/life."

These days, I laugh at the things I find humorous as opposed to what tickles a drinker's funny bone, a major sign of maturity for me.

Poor Mom, I joined a different religion from hers. But I am just as fervent about it. So as not to offend Mom's feelings, I waited until she had no sensibilities left (i.e. she was dead). I was a good daughter in my own way.

On a daily basis, I find myself keeping up Mom's traditions with my own particular slant. I laugh a lot (Laughter Yoga), sing loud and often (to Buddha in my temple choir, but I belt it out with passion, just the way she did), and tell funny stories. I am a good hostess to my Book club, Writer's Group and my son's friends. I gladly prepare abundant sustenance—though it's food rather than drink—for all of the above. Best of all, I no longer wonder what I missed in Mom's parties.

Chapter 7
Hall of Mirrors

I walk sideways with arms outstretched, waving here and there for balance, like a large praying mantis using its antennae. My feet walk on angled glass, so I slip and glide on shadows. But I am accustomed to walking among shady illusions and my feet bend easily to odd angles on the shimmery slope. After all, I am an artist and have lived in the art world for many years. In my mind's eye, I can see in every detail a scene of a thousand leaping grasshoppers on top of a cupcake, then paint them. Among my fellow artists, this ability is as natural as eating. So it does not seem odd to live in my preferred realities: that my mother loved me and that my ex-boyfriends were faithful to me. I achieved great success in believing these illusions for decades, but I received almost no recognition for my painted cupcakes and grasshoppers. Regardless, I continued to believe and to paint.

45

But one day, while sliding on slanted glass through a narrow hallway, I come upon a mirror that shows me to be short and plump as a gnome. No matter how high I stretch, I stay squat. I laugh, for I am a tall person of normal weight. But a voice in my head calls me a fat slob and tells me everything that goes wrong is my fault. No matter how intensely I keep myself distracted with grasshoppers, cupcakes and, later, my paintings of crickets on tiramisu, I believed the ugly voice for more than half of my life.

Around the next corner, when I gaze in a different mirror, I see my body in a wavy pattern. My face peers at me on the right side, but both shoulders are on the left. My stomach is on the right, knees to the left. My feet hold this balanced bodily contraption up from the right side. I look like a painted Picasso lady and feel like her for I am good at contorting myself in every possibly way to please my mother and boyfriends, no matter how extreme their demands grow. But I bend to their will while keeping my pride because I never stop painting my grasshoppers, cupcakes, crickets, tiramisu and later, mitochondria on macaroons.

When I turn around to a new mirror, I look like a waterfall in a drought, a floor to ceiling skinny, yet sparkling, white froth. At last I have lost enough weight. Now I am perfect, but hardly there, a wraith with my true self hidden; the way my mother and boyfriends prefer me to be. But I silently resist them with the canvases I place on the walls of my home deifying my beloved grasshoppers, cupcakes, crickets, tiramisu, mitochondria, macaroons and later, protozoa on pancakes with lots of syrup; not just the standard maple but also savory raspberry sauce and blue agave.

Now I laugh at my distortions in the mirrors. But for most of my life, I dearly loved the delusions my ego craved and created. I believed they were real; more real than my painted grasshoppers, cupcakes, crickets, tiramisu, mitochondria, macaroons, protozoa, pancakes, colored syrups, and lately, nano-engines on lemon squares.

Chapter 8
Ancestor Bias

I hate golf and am the most recent in a long lineage of golf-haters, generations of my socialist ancestors who came to this country to found a utopia free of golf and its class system. They established a socialist community in the rain forests of the Olympic Peninsula, hewing logs to build a theater that was the foundation of their educational system which taught that all humans were equal, all races, and all males and females within these races. In 1880, this was considered radical. As the spawn of such distinguished and liberated individuals, I thought myself free of prejudice, but in late adulthood, two of my ancestors' unsuspected biases came around full circle to haunt me.

I first realized the depth of my inherited golf prejudice when I bought a small anonymous-looking beige stucco townhouse adjacent to a golf course. My ancestors' strong opinions flew

49

out of the ether each time I looked at the second tee to see the plaid shorts and bright collared knit shirts stenciled in an upright Nike-shaped swoosh position, or sometimes a pony. Not only do I live "on a golf course," but I live in a sterile, regulated, immaculately groomed, gated community.

This brings me to ancestor prejudice number two: their pioneer history. I grew up to be proud of idealist great-grandparents and grandparents who built their log cabins on homestead land after the socialist community suffered financial failure, some family members having been not that good with numbers. They struggled to survive in the dark forests, farming near the large rivers, lakes and streams that dot the Pacific Northwest. They fished and hunted and farmed. I was dishonoring their memory by living in a fenced community in a drab townhouse, cheek to jowl with hundreds of other "little boxes made of ticky-tacky" situated around a desert golf course.

I have a very good excuse for choosing dull but safe anonymity: I wanted to escape a strange ex-boyfriend. But plenty of my cousins have weird exes, and they have kept to their pioneering ways, living and farming in rustic settings come what may. Even the city cousins have huge yards or acres where they keep chickens and grow their own food. They feel sorry for me, a shallow, culturally deprived anomaly. A "petty bourgeoisie."

To overcome these ancient prejudices, I have prepared a Manifesto of My New Self. Now hear this, ancestors and living relatives:

Like the female pheasant, I may be dull on the outside, but I have a powerful interior and can fly. Like you, dear relatives, I cut and slash raw materials from nature to make a living, but my resources are in my quiet home and come from my inner nature, exploding with emotion and acts of power that roar within my interior.

I hereby announce kinship to the bristlecone pine, the oldest being on earth that grows in the mountains near me. Most of the tree trunk and branches from base to crown look craggy and dead. They look like lumps of weathered browns. But near the ground, bushy foliage lives and grows. Like the 4000-year-old bristlecone, my exterior may look bland, but I am well-flushed and green near my roots. I don't have to look good or conform to family expectations to thrive.

I proclaim my authentic self to be the one you shall see henceforth. I am a pioneer explorer of my creative interior. I visit my rustic inner nature in meditation, in self-reflection, in painting and in writing, hewing down trees of illusion and self-deception to plant and water new life filled with self-regard. Although I don't live on a lake or in a forest, my ancestors would recognize me if they could see inside me and disregard the superficial stucco townhouse on the golf course. I can't see this happening anytime soon with the living, but maybe a few dead ones can see my inner work and cheer me on.

I hereby promise to keep true to my proclamations in good faith and good heart, carrying it under my arm wherever I go, vigilant about my prejudices.

Lately my friend Melissa, for example, alerted me to biases concerning rituals and emotions surrounding death. I have known Melissa for many decades; we have both lived in the arid Nevada desert for years, friends to cactus, sage, chaparral and to each other. She is now in her seventies and I am not far behind. The other day, she shocked me by saying, "I plan to die in Missouri where I grew up." My mouth fell open. She is perfectly healthy.

Although I work in hospice and often face the realities of death, I hadn't considered that I would have much choice about the exact spot of my demise. Like many today, I travel a lot and could drop dead anywhere. Had I overlooked a major life decision? Should I be orchestrating my death scene right now? I asked her more about it; she had lived in Nevada since her teenage years and her parents are buried there. She had enjoyed a very good career in the state with many close friendships and two husbands. But I discovered that she, like many people I know, has a bias against Nevada's bright lights. And honestly, do I want to have my memorial service in an Elvis Chapel that does spur-of-the-moment weddings? I could understand; when it comes to the bedrock values, the final comeuppance of death, Nevada is too glitzy for Melissa. Missouri is her real home in her heart and she wants to go home to die. She bought a house there, and moving day is imminent. But in the past year, we have talked about her feelings and her transition; she has been a great mirror for me.

I can't help but ask myself, "Why don't I want to die in Washington where I grew up and where my venerable ancestors pioneered? At age sixty-five, perhaps I should think about it. But, honestly, it never occurred to me and maybe this is one of those serious life questions I forgot to ask. Like, for example, how do you marry a nice person? Since it only occurred to me to answer that question late in life, I decide to seriously ponder Melissa's thoughts.

This year, when I went to Washington for family gatherings, I smelled the deep forest mosses and the sweet rotting fir and pine needles. They filled my lungs with nutrients rich as cedar ice cream. I thought, yes, I could die with these aromas nurturing my journey to the far world. I heard the eagles' cries and felt the soft gray moist air cover me like Grandmother Burns' silky handmade afghan. Yes, I could die with these cries in my ears and with this softness on my skin. I strolled out on a long pier into Puget Sound, as if I could walk straight into the arms of Hurricane Ridge, clear and snowy, the surrounding water green as Alaskan jade. I felt my father's presence so strongly that I asked him to help my cousin George on his death journey that had unexpectedly happened a couple days before. Tears poured from my eyes, no doubt glistening like the waters and the snows around me. My pioneer ancestors had felt, smelled and seen all of this in common with me. Yes, I could die with this closeness to them and to the iridescent colors that could lead me to the other shore.

Have I convinced myself to move to Washington for my death? No, I'm not like Melissa. But, at my age, I know the ultimate winds of impermanence will blow my direction sooner, rather than later. However, the sacred space within me is sanctified wherever I am: Washington, Hawaii, Nevada or points in between. The crash of warm ocean waves or the huge moon filling a desert valley or the dry air at 40,000 feet above earth would all be just as holy at my moment of death. Of course, my ego softly murmurs, "But you really hope for the moon or the ocean or Hurricane Ridge."

I admit you are right, ego. But I imagine, as I die, all the Buddhas will rush forward and hold me in their arms, and they will be the big reality, not recycled airplane air.

As Melissa packs her car for the long drive to Missouri, I ponder her situation. She kept her Nevada driver's license as proof of her Nevada "residence," so she'll be back and forth. And just before she hit the road with three cats, one dog and a trailer, news of a one-bedroom condo for sale at a good price in the Las Vegas Country Club brought a twinkle to her eye. "Hurray, you'll be back, Melissa. To see you again, I won't have to go to Missouri," I said. What I didn't say was, if she bought that condo, she would increase her chances of dying in Sin City after all.

Melissa inspires me to get more specific about where I will die and to wonder if I care, or whether my ancestors care. I visit Washington twice a year, so I have an eight percent chance of dying there. That's good enough for me. Deal with it, relatives and ancestors. I'll stick to my desert ticky-tacky and my inner cultivations of joy. Eventually, I can imagine I won't care if my family pities me for my superficial lifestyle.

I was happy when my son took up golf. "It's a fun and social sport," he said as I helped him move into an urban high rise apartment.

"Good for you," I replied as I praised his new home without uttering a word of old family biases.

Chapter 9
Unrequited-itis

One of my first memories was of running away. Apparently, I have always wanted to escape my family. In drippy Tacoma, I remember carefully donning my pink rain slicker and boots and hefting a bundle tied to a stick over my shoulder (pre-backpack days). Dad was still alive, so I was less than eight years old as I slipped down our long driveway to seek my fortune. I hoped an Indian tribe would adopt me as I favored the Indians over the cowboys in my books. But I had no idea where to find an Indian, so I wandered around the large lake across the street; perhaps one might be found in a canoe.

By evening, wet, cold and unadopted, I trudged back up our hill. No one in the family—two older sisters, arguing mother and father—perceived my absence. But each time I ran away, I always fruitlessly hoped someone might notice my escapes.

The dominant theme of my growing years was an eager

anticipation of being seen, and I tried all the likely tactics: starring in performances no family member ever attended, winning contests at school, catching bizarre diseases, repeated truancy. My family seemed afflicted with terminal distraction as far as I was concerned.

A healthy person would give up on them. But not me. By age eighteen, I ran away on a larger scale, off to Europe on my own (after working three jobs and saving every penny). I'd given up on Indian tribe adoption but hoped to fall in love with European nobility, marry and live happily ever after. That would show them that I had been an important person all along; they just hadn't seen the real me. But try as I might, no nobles appeared on bended knee. After a year, I landed back in Tacoma to finish college at the only school I could afford.

To make matters worse, I recently met a woman who had done the same as I at age eighteen. But she met the Swede of her dreams, married him and lived in Sweden for seventeen years; close enough to my fairy tale desires to inspire extreme jealousy, decades later.

Meanwhile back in Tacoma, my family had run away from me. Mom moved to Los Angeles and rented out our house. Both sisters had flown the coup, one to Baltimore and the other to Nepal with the Peace Corps. By moving back to Tacoma, I was free of family once more.

The trouble was, I still wanted them to notice me; it was like a chronic disease that I might have named Unrequited-itis if I had had enough awareness to realize this underlying affliction. When the family members eventually returned to the Tacoma area, I tried to gain their esteem by taking up with men I knew would pique their interest; that worked nicely for the men, but not for me.

In a modified escape, I moved a thousand miles away and had a child. At last my family poured forth esteem—well, mostly for my child, but it counted. When I visited home, Mom cuddled my son. My sisters included him in their activities.

I discovered another good way to draw family attention was to divorce. Although Mom was mortified and one sister remained distracted no matter what I did, the other sister had been through the devastating process and offered her support and friendship to me. At age fifty-five, one out of three was sweet.

Maybe that was enough or maybe, in old age, I finally outgrew my case of Unrequited-itis. I stopped escaping as a way to demand notice. Life became light with fully requited joy in my adult son.

But I now live 3,000 miles away from my family, a sort of permanent escapist contingency.

Chapter 10
Birth Souvenir

I applied for Medicare online and eagerly awaited the Social Security Administration's response. I naturally feared my name had disappeared into deep cyberspace. When Evelyn, a kind young-sounding SSA employee called me, I was thrilled. I was not lost, I was found. Unfortunately, she called to report a "discrepancy" in my birth place. As my stomach dropped several inches, I thought of Mom. All of my life, she had told me and whoever was nearby, that I was born in Washington, DC. I believed that my mother would know where I was born and I entered Washington DC as my birthplace on forms and in my psyche for five decades. To be fair, Dad worked in the nation's capital for several years around the time of my birth, and I guess she wanted to remind whoever was listening and all future bureaucrats who saw my papers of this fact.

When the passport office began to require a "certified" birth certificate after 9-11, I embarked on a search. Our address at the time of my birth was lost to history, as were Mom and Dad who had passed away. But, in Mom's papers I uncovered a form emblazoned with the words, Birth Certificate, across the top, featuring my two inked baby feet. At one point, I had tried to enter Canada with this document, only to be informed it was "not real" but a "souvenir" of my birth. Popping into the world must have been so much fun, I waved my tiny arms and demanded a memento before I left Disney hospital.

However, my birth souvenir reported my origins in Cheverly, Maryland, at Prince George's hospital. At least I knew which state to apply for the certified birth certificate, U.S. government approved. For the past several years, I had begun entering Cheverly, Maryland, in the birth place slot on forms. Although I had moved away at one year old and had no memory of the place, it was a comfort to know my real origins. I had begun to identify with my city of birth and planned to visit someday. Luckily, I obtained this document a few years back, which I proudly reported to Evelyn. She sounded happy indeed, probably relieved to avoid the souvenir birth certificate explanation to one more disgruntled customer. "Good for you. All you have to do now," she said, "is take the certified birth certificate to your SSA office and show it to them so we can clear up your discrepancy." What a relief. The SSA could finally fix my lifetime of accidental lies.

Having visited federal bureaucracies before, I planned an all-day excursion, taking a thick book by my favorite romance author (in a plain brown wrapper), a sure-fire sedative. Surrounded by twitchy teenagers on three sides and a loud baby behind me, I happily lost myself for hours in Lord and Lady Belvedere's bedroom dramas. When I heard my number called at last, I was cheery and stimulated.

And disconcerted to arrive at Window Eleven and sit before someone I recognized but could not place. I had accomplished a major feat of organization when I planned this trip, carrying five file folders of every conceivable type of documentation and identification. Now I stared across this wash of papers, wondering why I knew this attractive middle-aged Asian woman. She stared at me, too. I pushed over some papers, unaware of what they were. All I could say was, "You look so familiar." She shuffled through my paperwork.

"Maybe our kids were in school together," she said, staring at my papers, "but your son had a different last name." She also muttered something else, but, the older I got, the more people mumbled. I was getting used to it, but I was sure she had not said, "Go out and take some air," which is what it sounded like. I supplied my son's full name and the world clicked into place when she said her daughter's name: Molly. In fact, I clearly remembered her from kindergarten as the very cute girl who had trouble in the lavatory one day and returned to class with her pants around her ankles. When I asked what Molly was doing now, I learned she was in medical school.

I continued to frantically search for the application I had carefully filled out beforehand. "I can't find the application," I said with an apology in my voice.

"Oh, you already handed it to me," she said. I was more discombobulated than I had thought.

"Oh, sorry. I'm a little flustered. Can you remind me of your name?"

"Claire," she said.

"Oh," I said. "I was just thinking of the name, Claire." Then I felt a dread certainty, she must have "mumbled" her name when I first sat down. Between that and the application confusion, I had just proved my need for Medicare. But I also remembered that I had really liked Claire, her husband and daughter. We had been room mothers together, an "in the trenches" bonding. As she processed paper after paper, we caught up on our lives. I admired her multitasking skills as she attacked several machines to correct my discrepancy. She was producing a miracle: hope that my mother's lies would not follow me to the grave.

I had noticed that my certified birth certificate did not list my city of birth as Cheverly; it only stated the county. Prince George's County. I brought this up with Claire and she, a fount of bureaucratic precision, said she could only submit what was on the U. S. government certified birth certificate. So, my birth place changed again: It became Prince George's. I was seized with instant self-pity and jealously for my two big sisters who were born in real cities: Vancouver and Olympia. They have always known where they were born and have a lifetime of consistent documents to prove it. Now I had to change my birth place a third time. It wasn't fair. They had all the advantages. I was now born in Prince George's; it is not even grammatically correct unless I add "county." (Did Prince George own the county at one time?) They don't have to say Vancouver city or Olympia city. Henceforth, all my forms must say Prince George's County as my birth place. My poor emotions can't bend to embrace. this awkward grammar as a place I can identify with, as a place to be proud of, as a place to visit. Later, my son pointed out an advantage; being born in a county gives me instant redneck credibility, something I can use in everyday life if I work on my backwoods' accent.

"Now," she said, after amazing feats on multiple fronts, "you should be able to claim your award within sixty days." I must have looked confused. My "award"? I was so needy to "win" prizes, I have been known to purchase ten or more raffle tickets to boost my chances. Winning was pure delirium. But, the Social Security Administration would give me "an award"? I thought Medicare was health insurance. In a few years, I planned to submit a claim for the Social Security money I had already paid during decades of work. I acutely remembered those deductions of much-needed cash on each paycheck. But part of me, the childlike part the Social Security Administration counted on to love getting a prize, was, in reality, slowly returning to childhood and couldn't wait to get my "award." Oh boy.

Chapter 11
Learn the Hard Lessons

In high school—the prime drug years—whenever my son acquired a new friend I hadn't met, I worried. Was this the druggie who would lead my son down the black path, ruin him and display my parental failure to the world?

Thus, when he started to spend time with Felix, I was anxious. Especially on the night my son, a serious eater, didn't show up for dinner. Earlier in the day he told me he and Felix were meeting after school. From 3 p.m. to 8 p.m., I reprimanded myself, "Don't hover." "Let him learn the hard lessons on his own." Meanwhile, my fingernails disappeared as I gnawed on them. I was certain Felix, a year older than my son in the same Honolulu high school, was inducting him into the downtown drug world and, at that moment, was demonstrating how to find a vein.

Around 9 p.m., my son arrived home. In my best "I trust

you, son" voice, I casually wondered where he had been.

"Oh," he said, "Felix took me to dinner with his parents at the Pacific Club."

My eyes lost focus as I stammered, "Wha...? How?" The private exclusive Pacific Club was for Honolulu's elite.

"Oh, didn't I ever tell you? Felix's last name is Halawa."

My knees wobbled with surprise. The Halawa family was famous in town for owning banks and being CEOs of the largest business around. Both parents were regularly quoted in the news and included on the annual top salaries list: one for her (always at the top) and one for him. My son went from street person to hobnobber in one second.

During the next year, my son's friends were close to his age and my worry gauge turned low. But a year later, his new friend Jake, a slick Elvis type, troubled me again. Jake was several years younger. What would bond them except drugs?

In my day, upper and lower classmen didn't mingle. We remained grade-monogamous. A senior hanging out with a junior was suspicious. Was such a senior retarded (we used the R-word in those days)? I applauded my son's high school's approach that mingled grades nine through twelve in all classes, college style. For example, an English class might contain freshmen, sophomores, juniors and seniors all together. But my old prejudices about grade-monogamy lurked in subterranean cranial passages and jumped out in unexpected panic now and then.

After several months of their friendship, one day, my son announced he and Jake were going to the other end of the island to visit a friend of Jake's, a full day's trip.

"Oh," I said supportively, with secret suspicions. "Who is that?"

My son's green eyes sparkled with excitement. "It's the earl."

"Is that someone's name?" I asked, but wondered if it was drug slang or a ghetto pop reference, as in the song, "Duke of Earl."

"No, it's the Earl of Sherwood."

My brain couldn't compute this fact. We live on a tiny island in the middle of the Pacific half a world away from real earls in Britain. I shook my head. "Huh?"

As it turns out, the true Earl of Sherwood (yes, he is genuine, but of course, I changed his name) owns a house on the north end of Oahu; his son was a surfing enthusiast. Through the surfing community, Jake's dad became close to the earl's son and eventually to the earl. They often visit when the earl is on the island. The next day, my son reported that the earl was a quiet, regular guy with white skinny legs in shorts.

I have officially given up suspecting my son and his friends of drug addiction. His friends far outrank me now and I'm happy to cling to their, and my son's, coattails.

Medicine Wheel East
Male Amazements

On the traditional Native American medicine wheel, the East is the place of the mind, reflecting wisdom, mental work and concepts. In the human life cycle, the age that most represents this direction is the wise elder, a person who can detach from circumstances with love, stay focused on the task at hand and see beyond the obvious.

The East is also the home of the Native American "heyoka," the sacred clown or court jester, always teasing and poking fun at established institutions and the status quo to test their validity, with the ultimate goal of increasing our wisdom (or killing us).

In my world, the court jesters who have tested me and my bedrock beliefs the most are men. Somehow, these relationships go topsy-turvy and never turn out to be what any logical person would have expected. I dedicate the East to the men who have been in my life.

Chapter 12
Libido Tsunami

I had just returned home from a blissful spiritual retreat with lots of meditation. During the final days, we women had explored our inner male qualities. Old news, I thought. In most of my relationships, I was the one who changed the oil in our car and made carpentry repairs to the house. I was no simpering female. My inner male was alive and well. I hadn't been in a relationship for years, but I managed my own household doing both the male and female tasks, just as I always had.

When I got home from the retreat, I noticed that my sex drive gave a small leap for no apparent reason. At my age, it's not what I expected. Most retirees focus on knee and hip replacements; I thank the joint gods I've—so far—avoided that. As a single woman for ten years, I'd noticed that this time of life did not provide a lot of dates. My hiatus from males was actually a relief after decades of taking care of and being abused by this man or the other.

But those subtle sensual pleasures in the Second Chakra inexplicably continued to grow, week by week. Soon I began to fidget, even in loose clothing. While reading a book or having breakfast, enjoyable thudding sensations in my nether regions pounded on a regular basis. Throughout the day, they took on a life of their own. Something down there squirmed and grew! I feared that everyone could see whatever creature moved around below my waist; I now empathized with teenaged boys' self-consciousness. I noticed my brain function decreased concerning topics unrelated to sex. The moving thing in my pants continued to grow, albeit in a pleasant way, but soon sleep was difficult. Was I building up to the rare sexual Tourette's syndrome I'd read about where a woman breaks out in spontaneous orgasms at work or in the grocery store?

Enter Brian, soft-spoken accountant retiree. He had all his hair, most of it still black. We had met months before, but he had a girlfriend. Now he didn't, or rather, kind of didn't. He was at the end of a break-up, but still in a sensitive stage. I decided to keep a polite distance; pecks on the cheek upon greeting and leave-taking, though even those chaste salutations sent my writhing jeans into double-speed throbbing.

Brian and I kept arranging to meet on what turned out to be a daily basis. When, one evening, we both missed the cheek-kiss and ended up mouth to mouth, a raw chemistry exploded that I hadn't felt in decades and never expected to feel again. The quiet, retired CPA was an adept French kisser. All the old clichés kicked in as my knees went soft and I weakened into a speechless feminine swoon, my breath ragged. And the sensations down below grew above my waistline; my enlarged organ felt like it was waving like a Venus flytrap on the hunt.

Brian held me up while I regained my balance and asked with a frown, "Are you okay?"

I gamely smiled though heaving lungs. "It's not a heart attack, I just liked your kiss." "Liked" was an understatement. But I wasn't sure how much to explain. I only hoped my clothes covered my private parts which were creeping up almost to my chest. However, neither of us could stop at one kiss and by the time we got to my apartment parking lot, we were making out like teens; I hoped the building security guards weren't watching on their cameras. And like during my high school years, we both stopped at first base in unspoken agreement. We parted, panting, and I literally staggered alone into my building, stunned, holding my arms across my stomach.

Inside, I fell into bed, afraid to look in the mirror. My female parts felt like they were growing up my neck, breathing in a delightful rhythm that bore no relation to my conscious command. Every thought of Brian sent the tissues into shudders and piercing vibrations. It's a good thing I'd always believed my feminine core was clean and beautiful. But enough was enough. Perhaps it would shrink back to normal size by tomorrow?

It didn't.

The next morning, my face looked the same (albeit with a silly grin), but the rest of me was a full walking vagina, lit up with a glowing iridescent warm light. When dressed in a turtleneck and long pants, I blended in with a crowd. I did my errands, and no one seemed to notice my slight stagger, for whenever I thought of Brian, my gigantic female region would swell. It felt like everyone on the street must have been able to see my raw and florescent state.

For several days, I walked around with my essential being wide open to the world, vulnerable in the most private way. Knowing that the Sacral Plexus Chakra was the foundation of emotions, sexuality, ability to get along with others, creativity and a place of connection to Mother energies where we were deeply in touch with our bodies, I was the living essence of the ancient Great Mother deity. But what the heck was going on? I just wanted to kiss a guy, not be anyone's archetypal female idol.

This was an Art Historical emergency. I thumbed through my Art History books to find the medieval stone carvings I remembered. There she was! I closely resembled the Sheela Na

Gig, who suffered from the same physical state as me. She was carved into gateways and doors leading into cathedrals. Nude, she crouched and exposed her giant genitalia, which she grabbed on each side and pulled apart to reveal all. At least I hadn't gone that far yet. In this way, she protected the cathedral portals and gates from evil spirits with what was, after all, the ultimate gateway: the birth canal. She was mostly created in Ireland and until the early twentieth century, there were documented observations of living Sheela Na Gig women who would terrorize an enemy by impersonating the stone statue. This says a lot about the Irish. But what enemy was *I* chasing away?

I didn't have to look far for an answer. I've never met a man I could trust. From father to boyfriends, I was fair game for violence and abandonment. And now in my life, there appeared a hunk who kick-started my engine. Could I trust him? My intuition (which I consulted about six times a day) said, "Yes."

And my Sheela Na Gig body said, "Yes, for I am protecting you with my great woman-powers."

When I realized fate gave me a chance to learn how to trust male energy for the first time, I waddled forth to see Brian each day. We had agreed to be mature adults and remain celibate for a while to give us time to get to know each other. He needed time to recover from a recent break-up. And after some bad relationships of my own, I didn't want to jump into a new relationship without knowing the man really well. But that message hadn't gotten through to my dominant anatomical feature which continued its relentless intense routine. In an ultimate test of my willpower, Brian and I spent time each day talking, eating, walking, watching the sunset, laughing, and kissing. When I hugged those hard shoulders, I thought my colossal organ might reach out and absorb all of Brian in one big gulp, like a crazed *femme fatale*. But it didn't. One day at a time, as the twelve-step programs suggested, I stayed the course and kept my ravenous lust in her place. I wondered if this hormonal aberration was permanent and I would remain an enriched super vagina well into my nineties.

At home, I thought peaceful meditation might calm my tempestuous urges and correct my physical anomaly. But quiet contemplation brought visions of Tantric *Yab Yum* sacred union and Kama Sutra sex, which, by ethereal grace, surged through me almost continuously. Even in meditation, my brain stayed fixated on the great mysterious generative process. Females produced life, the ultimate in creativity.

I was attempting something new and enormous for me: the possibility of trust in a man. According to ancient Hawaiian kahuna belief, this was a personal realignment of the vital *KaneWahine* (male-female) spiritual basis of all life into its most potent balance, one of aloha.

At last the light dawned. This libido tsunami was a rite of

passage. If I was to truly come to trust male energy, I had to first become engulfed and wholly (holy) present in the female. I was given the gift of high creative energy that I could use to transform myself.

After a week of regular discipline—acting as if I were an ordinary woman and keeping to my inner commitment not to jump on this near stranger—my out-of-control craving began to slowly recede and my female privates shrank, bit by bit, from neck-height down to chest-level. For the next few days, the unhurried tide continued to go out bit by bit. I was sorry to see it ebb. I missed the storm surges of feeling and tempestuous moods that had kept me on the edge.

My capris fit comfortably now. Brian set my blood racing when I often thought of him. But my female parts remained firmly placed in their usual geographical location. However, they were now layered and complex with corporal and spiritual meaning: Second Chakra balance of openness and emotion, Great Mother energetic depths, Sheela Na Gig protection, *Femme Fatale* abilities of absorption, Kama Sutra transcendence, *Yab Yum* union, *KaneWahine* aloha, ultimate creativity. All had entered me in an intensely physical process, an initiation into their raw powers. From their original massive proportions, they had taken their time to gradually absorb into the tissue, blood and bones of my Second Chakra core. I had allowed myself to fully feel and name each part of the experience as it happened, and now I could claim it as my own, allowing my inner female strength to balance with male energies in aloha.

Chapter 13
A Good Man

Unfortunately, in the fullness of time, I came to realize my CPA had apparently not taken any ethics courses; the ex-girlfriend he had assured me was very "ex," was not actually an "ex." But this revelation allowed me to maintain my perfect track record: I haven't had relationships with any good men. However, I remember fantasizing about a handsome sweetheart in the past and trying to force my illusions to come true.

Recently, a friend fell in love, and her Facebook page became gooey with all the typical lovey-dovey scenes of kissing and staring into each other's eyes in a soulful stupor. Why wasn't she embarrassed by the stereotypical excess? She reminded me of myself years ago when I believed in the Romantic Ideal; at that time, I did as the New Age pundits recommended and made lists of the characteristics my ideal man should have. I had nice romances with lovely men who met all the requirements, but, probably due to my poor list-making skills, they either:

1. Beat me up

2. Carried on with others behind my back

They gave me a huge and abiding appreciation for a quiet, peaceful and solitary life, which explains why the only good man I can now imagine is the Bodhisattva Avalokiteshvara, the Great Buddha of Compassion.

On the earthly level, the two Tibetan lamas I study with come as close to Avalokiteshvara as you can get. These lamas are very human. I have seen the older lama sob with grief for his parents' sudden deaths and the fact that he never got to tell them good-bye. And I have seen the younger lama get angry at people who wanted to pay less money at the garage sale we had (he thought they were cheating). And one time, he got very annoyed at me for my selfish attitude. He was right, but I was shocked at his sudden anger. But these deeply human qualities allow me to see how they genuinely accept their emotions, and, with love and understanding, proceed with life's daily tasks. Having been with the lamas for the past fourteen years has allowed me to see this process over and over. Plus, they have a terrific sense of humor and we laugh a lot—an essential quality in a good man. And the lamas know how to fix anything; a man who repairs is divine.

But they are men in skirts. Using the lamas as my example

of male integrity begs the question: Does a good man have to be sex-less? I love sex, but have not experienced a good man who has sex with me. Although all is peachy when the relationship starts, after a while, I find sex stimulates a man's "Gimme, gimme" response, a scientific term meaning "She's willing to give me her body, therefore, she must be willing to give me her bank account, her car, her soul."

Which in turn, stimulates my enabling female, "Yes, I will give you my body, bank account, car and soul."

But I concede that a good male sexual partner may exist. My friend Hannah's common-law husband, Will, might be a good man. She doesn't officially marry him due to her past experiences similar to mine of the "Gimme, gimme/Enabling" syndrome. Will has been married three or four times; apparently, he was not always a good man, but he is now. He is a tall, handsome blond with piercing blue eyes and a scar across his cheek that adds to his masculine mystique. He enjoys a good belly laugh and can fix anything that will hold still long enough. He gives Hannah backrubs and loves to do all the things she does; they travel and explore nature, build houses and play card games. He took great care of her mother in her last years.

Because of Will I believe that a good man who also likes healthy sex can exist. However, it took Will several poor marriages to reach this point. I seem to attract men in the trainee stages, which leaves the lamas looking great.

Chapter 14
Behind Puppy Eyes and Sauce Stealing

Due to technical difficulties (discouragement in relationships and the healing time required afterward), I skipped sex for a decade during my prime, from 2004 to 2014. Like a traveler who has lived abroad for ten years, I returned to the American sexual landscape and did not recognize my own country.

During this seminal era, millions of ordinary people had been inundated with online porn. These same folks had watched TV shows like *Sex and the City*, where casual sex was the norm. Ditto for movies and TV news where gratuitous sex paired with violence increased the publics' ever-escalating sensation-quotient. I was never a big TV or porn watcher, so I also missed this cultural phenomenon.

A product of the liberated 1960s and 1970s, I was no prude. But at the time I went celibate, women had the right to say yes or no to sex, and the man accepted the woman's decision without question: a cultural norm that I believe derived from the anti-macho "sensitive man" era, an offshoot of hippy times. No more. Now men expect casual sex and when told "No" respond in one of the following ways:

• He replies that when a woman says "No," she means "Yes." Therefore he ignores my decision. This myth is a holdover from old misogynist days, surfacing once more in porn dogmas.

• He gives me puppy eyes, gazing at my face, hoping to alchemically change my brain to mush. When I persist with "No," I've learned the big goofy look is the prelude to anger, and each one is equally manipulative, the puppy-eyed man and the angry man both attempting to take something from me.

• "But it's the second date" (meeting for coffee, each driving separately, and deciding to get something to eat with the coffee apparently qualifies as "a date" if he pays). "Second date" now means, "I can put my hands anywhere on your body." A "No" elicits puppy eyes, or anger, or an astounded "Wow, are you kidding?" meaning, "What's wrong with you?" or "What century are you from?"

Like I said, I missed a decade. I can't help but notice a trend of macho impulsiveness on the rise.

But this may be part of a larger cultural trend that I have

recently observed: sauce stealing. When my friends rented a house for a couple of weeks near where I live, I became the recipient of bags of groceries they hadn't used by the time of their departure. In the bags were dozens of bottles and plastic containers of the sauces and condiments found on restaurant tables: catsup, honey, hot sauce, jams, peanut butter. Stolen goods.

My son recently reported a friend in possession of a large bottle of hot sauce when they were out on the town clubbing. When asked why he was carrying the hot sauce, his buddy replied in a casual voice, "It's from the restaurant where we just ate."

And a friend told me about a gathering in a restaurant, where a member of the group took a full-sized bottle of catsup and put it in her purse. A large cross-section of unrelated folks of all ages and living in various states think it's okay to steal sauces; this amounts to a zeitgeist, and I am shocked.

What does this have to do with casual sex? One word: grasping. Wanting your sauce and eating it, too. Stealing honey is not unlike bullying to get sex. A hedonistic threshold level is at the tipping point in our society where we automatically indulge our appetites, regardless of ethical or health concerns. Need I mention America's Great Fattening in the past decade?

Why epidemic grasping at the killer level? Certainly it can destroy a fat body and it can stop a tender budding relationship.

Why now?

Perhaps the baby boomer generation demands one last hedonistic pleasure as part of its various bucket lists, whether Ben and Jerry's, porn or drugs; it's easy to blame everything on the boomers. I am one, subject to all the permissive appetites of my generation. But I happened to skip a decade of the social sexual scene, rendering me sensitive to the new mores.

Perhaps electronic media weakens our moral core and make society more impersonal, our online presence gaining importance over relationships with real people. Studies on the over-stimulation of porn (reliant on relationships with photographs and videos rather than with flesh-and-blood complex personalities) show that it deadens sexual response over time. And not much time. Doctors now treat new hordes of young men in their twenties for erectile dysfunction. And maybe our rampant grasping is the result of the ancient human desire to get something for nothing, exaggerated by the abundance of our wealthy age and by global communication making everything—products and relationships—seem instantly available.

We are in an immense renaissance and social upheaval: new definitions of what a family is (marriage not required, but gay marriage accepted), modifications of gender roles, computer technology radically changing the job markets, wars and homeland terrorism in our daily consciousness, new products with innovative materials using green energies. Constant and rapid changes might well produce human desires to clutch at momentary pleasures: insensitive sex, petty thievery, overeating. I've been subject to them all, but when I am, it bothers me.

Rather late in life I found that many times a day, I can make a choice about where I place my mind; I can decide whether to have a greedy mind or not. A wise Tibetan lama told me: When I feel compelled by a sudden need, I can stop and ask the question, "At this moment, is it possible that the opposite can be equally true?" For example, when my mind says, "Grab that cookie," I can counter with, "Hmmm. Interesting. But what does my body really want right now?" Sometimes, my mind says, "To heck with it," and I snatch the sweets. But more often than I would suspect, my body tells my mind, "I prefer carrots." And I say, "Sure." The opposite of a cookie can be equally delicious. With the discovery of this possibility, I made a vow to respect what my body really wants, once I looked below the impulse. Like repeated physical workouts, over time this exercise becomes easier and second nature.

Lust is more difficult. When in the grip of sexual chemistry, the pull feels overwhelming; nature is brutal, hauling out all the chemical stops. And romance is a good thing, right? It's fun and provides meaning to life for many, especially my extroverted high-living Mom who collected double-digit fiancés on her

89

love belt of notches. She taught me well, but I never came close to her stellar achievements: my proposal tally equals one. However, I learned to follow the hormonal lure whenever it beckoned as a valued end in itself (as I have assumed for most of my life). But as I look back on my disastrous track record with men, I sense underlying currents that the wise lama's teaching encourages me to notice. Was it really true love when I was in college wanting to study law and I "fell in love" with a law professor? And could you call it love when, years later, I wanted to learn more about biology and I went head over heels into a relationship with a man who others called a "scientific genius?" My emotions felt true and real at the time, but even Mickey Mouse could perceive an underside in these situations, a grasping to compensate for my incompetence in the areas in which I strove. No surprise, these relationships ended badly.

Although I had not experienced a blast of sexual chemistry for many winters, recently, lust hit hard. I mentally cowered, wondering, "Oh no, what's on the underside of this one?" The lama's voice stayed with me. Could it be that, at age sixty-five, I was mistaking the ego boost of attraction for true love? Yes, probably. I kept this thought in mind while I rode the passion to its unsurprising conclusion, a prolonged and messy break up; my form of grasping, no doubt, not wanting to let the cute guy go.

If I am honest with myself, I am not above the grossest kind of grasping in its many forms. Luckily, I haven't wanted to shoplift in fifty years, not since getting caught as a teenager with resulting massive shame. Punishment and humiliation work as deterrents; this will be good to remember if another cute guy glances my direction.

Anger has never been my default emotion; mortification is my "go-to" setting. However, when anger sometimes strikes, I hate it. This suffering is much easier than lust to dissect because I want it to end now. As per the good lama's insight, when I turn over anger's rock, I usually find the bottom crawling with my illusions. "The hunk would never prefer his younger ex-girlfriend over me." Duh. When I face this stupid delusion, anger backs off a bit.

A friend is in the process of selling out a family inheritance so she can buy a larger yacht with full-sized appliances. Her current fifty-footer has a pint-sized stove and refrigerator. I nearly jumped on my moral high horse in disgust at her bourgeois values, but, I'm afraid the reality is that I get seasick in rough water and have no desire for any type of boat. She has reached her eighth decade and recently had a heart attack. Don't most of us lubricate hard realities with some indulgence? With a lot of indulgence, if we can afford it? I do, simply not with vehicles; they are not my particular temptation. Sex is. Food is. Ambition is. Delusions of desirability are. Stealing was. Seeing others' follies helps me to see my own.

I have moved from being shocked and appalled at others' flaws to realizing that I am part of the social trends and harbor my own human faults, subject to the same pressures. But I manage to say "No" some of the time. I don't steal sauces. And I listen to the lama as I muddle through each day, catching my mind in its endless tricks and justifications as best I can. I remain hopeful that the clutch of grasping won't choke me.

Chapter 15
Order in the Court

It seemed like a good idea to date a handsome bailiff. With large muscles, a sensitive boyish face, and a low-key demeanor, he was well worthy of my lust. Besides, I hadn't had a boyfriend in ten years. For a senior citizen who didn't trust the web lurkers, pickings were slim, so to find Joseph was a coup. We enjoyed a mutual infatuation. In an effort to be a mature adult and wait to get to know him before sex, I held out six weeks before I dragged him into bed. A rare man (in my experience) who truly enjoyed giving pleasure, he seemed to be sent directly from heaven.

The first time he mentioned handcuffs, I sincerely laughed; it must be a well-worn joke among law enforcement types who find themselves in romantic situations. I told him if he brought out the cuffs, I was history to him.

But the second time he brought up the subject, in drowsy

post-coital pillow talk, I came instantly alert. Like a cozy sales clerk, he pitched all of the benefits: that the cuffs were like a toy and we could play around with them, it would be so much fun, and I would love being ravished while helpless. I admit I loved the "ravished" part, but abhorred "helpless." Why he thought I would go for the whole package was a mystery. I made a mental note to examine our previous conversations more closely. All of my "No way!" and "Forget it!" responses inspired more salesmanship. Trying to stop him with a joke, I told him I would expect to handcuff him too; a comment he ignored. To end this topic once and for all, I sternly said, "I am an artist. My hands are my life. I don't give them away to anyone for any reason." The sales pitch stopped.

But a tiny voice in my mind wondered if handcuff-play might be fun. I'd never been one for sex toys, but a Brazilian girlfriend of mine loved them. Even in this pre "Fifty Shades of Grey" popularization of control-freak sex play, I wondered if I was out of touch with modern dating and was being closed-minded.

As if sensing my ambiguity, every once in a while over the next month, Joseph repeated the selling features of handcuffing me. He happened to have a pair in the car, available in a moment. He varied the theme by mentioning the virtues of being tied up with rope. In the intervening weeks, he must have noticed that I enjoyed talking about psychology, for he added the necessity of the deep trust essential between the handcuffer and the handcuffee. I began to consider it: play, fun, trust. What could be wrong with that?

After we made love the last time, he murmured in a sweet voice, "Wouldn't it be exciting to have a little pain, just enough to increase our excitement?" He seemed shocked at my protests. "But this would be love-pain," he explained as if it was a kind that didn't hurt.

The truth was, carnal relations with Joseph were more bestial than I'd ever experienced before and much to my surprise, a huge turn-on. Animal Kingdom 101, noisy and primeval, on the verge of pain; I now understood the Klingons. "You know, Joseph, what we're doing now is enough love-pain for me. This is new for me, and I love this intense stuff. But I don't want any more; that would be actual pain, and I've had enough of that in my life."

Joseph might have had a good point on the love-pain, but enough was enough. No cuffs or ropes for me. It was past time to clear things up.

I sat down with him for a serious pre-coital talk (on his lap, true, but no one is perfect). "Tell me what the deal is with handcuffs and being tied down. I need to know if you are joking or not."

He laughed in his winsome way. "Oh, yeah, it's just a way to tease you, honey. I can't believe you would get so worried about this."

But I remembered other playful conversations when I had asked him if he'd ever been tied or cuffed by someone else before. He'd said he didn't care for it very much as he found it claustrophobic. My suspicious mind thought his true mission might be to tease me into acquiescing to bondage. I figured this was a strong part of Joseph's fantasy life and had been for a long time. Time to be blunt.

"I need you to know that talking about cuffs and ropes is a big turn-off to me."

His eyes widened in surprise. "Really, sweetheart?" Then he grinned. "You mean you don't want to be ravished by me with your hands tied?"

I stared into his eyes. "Not my thing, buster."

"You know I would never hurt you, dear. But just having a little more pain would bring us both so much more excitement."

"Not for me. That's your fantasy."

His eyes twinkled with the game. "And you really don't want me to kiss you everywhere after I've cuffed you?"

I weakened. His kisses were extraordinary. But then I remembered the metal parts involved and my insides turned to steel. "That is not my need. It belongs to you, not me. Look, Joseph, I'm serious. If all those are important to you or if you need them, I'm the wrong one for you," I said.

Joseph laughed as if truly amused. "Sweetie, I don't need any of them. Those things would add a little bit of fun, that's all. But I won't mention them again if you don't want me to."

"Please don't. You are thrilling enough for me just the way you are. I don't need the extras," I said with a wiggle and a smooch.

Perhaps he meant it. But, when I thought about it and reached beneath layers of ego and lust, my intuition clearly saw that Joseph was a person who got what he wanted. I quit fooling myself and carefully planned my exit from his life.

Chapter 16
Male Scent

I had never craved the male scent before. In my mid-sixties, I noticed all my senses were slowly headed to the grave; thus said the optometrist, the audiologist, the dermatologist, and the gynecologist, using polite medical terms. But when I met Phil, I was like a wolf, following my nose into compelling crevices and crannies. I couldn't stop. Phil's pheromones provided a roadmap to an unknown land that I had to explore. To smell his world was to understand it. He seemed to like my doglike snuffling all over him.

When I inhaled Phil, I absorbed a nutrient essential to my health, vitamin X, a sexual sucrose; the more I drew in, the bigger hit I needed an hour later. Like Spice in the Dune novels, Vitamin X was highly addictive.

Why would nature give me a wolf nose and an overabundant passion for male musk at my age? Luckily, this compulsion did not apply to every male I saw or I would have been deranged from constant overstimulation; only Phil drew me in. As a result, I did not want to be without him. I needed my nasal fix. Was a grandparent range of bonding a Darwinian need to help raise any possible young children that might be around? If so, was this really so essential in the natural world that I needed to fixate on Phil's pheromones? I think not. It felt more like a hormonal malfunction, but one I was happy to indulge.

A raw and new experience, nothing in my romantic past had prepared me for this. It was as unexpected as seeing feet sprout out of my head. It made no evolutionary sense; I hadn't realized how reassuring Darwin's theories had been to me, providing a bedrock comprehension of life's whys and wherefores. Of course, I had committed stupid teenaged and early twenties dating mistakes, subject to a raw surfeit of estrogen without mature pre-frontal lobes, just as nature intended while she ruthlessly pressed me to reproduce. I could easily blame Mother Nature for my young blunders.

But, now I was an elder in a Darwin-be-damned state of mind. Should I know better? Were my aged, fully developed pre-frontal lobes withering away? I didn't care. In a delightful new olfactory frontier, I abandoned myself to the pure sensate wolf world, expanding my nostrils to comprehend exactly who Phil was and where he had been: at the beach, working out at the gym, drinking smoothies at the health food store, in the shower. I recognized it all. I marked him, streaking my sweat and saliva on his skin. So strong was my instinct, I was certain I could sniff out danger lurking around him. But I only inhaled a deep sense of belonging; he held the scent of our den, our home.

Apparently my intuition got carried away with limbic hedonism, and in good time, I made a discovery. If my special man had been one of nature's wild creatures I enjoyed living with, such as a pet gerbil, who I eventually learned had a pesky promiscuous tendency, I would have named him Phil, short for Philander. I concluded that even wolves made mistakes. Or perhaps the lesson here was simple: Canines loved the smell of rodents.

I returned again to Darwin's cold comfort: Survival of the Fittest. I have survived my wolf nose, therefore I must be fit. But I couldn't help but wonder: fit for what?

Chapter 17
Death Threat Etiquette

When walking into a crowded room and unexpectedly seeing a man who wants to kill you, a certain social awkwardness ensues, and I recommend the Rattlesnake Tactic.

But first, I want to thank you for attending my lecture today. I address a difficult, but under-appreciated social problem more prevalent than you might imagine in our increasingly global, networked society. Today there is more information than ever about where you are and when you are likely to appear at certain locations.

Yes, I understand this is a dreadful subject we would rather ignore: potential violence, a term which doesn't begin to describe this ultimate insult. In today's world, we do not have the luxury of ignorance, so my talk today focuses on survival after you have dealt with the fear, unfairness, and reality of your physical safety. You have the rest of your full, rich, immense life to live, and here is how you can best enjoy it.

Back to the crowded room with an unsavory guest. Before we employ the Rattlesnake Tactic, we must remove two basic concerns. We assume you have done your homework and you know the threat is real. Who knew that death threats have a rating system, like everything else in American life? Written murder plans are a ten, the most lethal because they are deliberate and cunning. A threat made "in the heat of passion" (to quote a law enforcement official) is only rated as a three. In the case of our man across a crowded room, whom I shall call "X," let's assume you've previously seen his written plans for your murder. The threat is therefore high, hence the social tension.

We'll next assume you have done Homework Assignment Number Two: taken all possible legal and common-sense steps to protect yourself. You have learned whether making his murder plans public or getting a restraining order would help or not. For the sake of our discussion, let's say that in X's case, either of these would make things worse. You have consulted with legal, security and domestic violence experts, have formulated a security plan and become accustomed to living by it. Let's assume that X has not yet been caught committing a crime, is free to wander and look like a good citizen, a common situation world-wide.

The Rattlesnake Tactic

Untoward social encounters may occur and when they do, the Rattlesnake Tactic is effective. Lock eyes with X. Slowly walk backward, continue an unblinking stare. Be silent. Show no fear. When out of striking range or in X's case, visual range, high-tail it. This strategy also works well with large predators. When facing a bulky animal, it helps to make oneself appear larger by swinging a large object, like a branch, above the head, hardly practical at a party. But squaring your shoulders, lifting your head and taking a deep breath will achieve a similar effect.

Another benefit of the Rattlesnake Tactic is that it saves face: It can be easily done in a busy area. Few people notice, as opposed to the ruckus caused if you scream wildly and run away.

The Pollyanna Plan

Perhaps you're standing at a party with a cocktail in hand, nervously flicking your eyes across the room at X, pretending that everything is fine. Do not underestimate the social pressure to act as if nothing is wrong, otherwise known as the Pollyanna Plan. But being in the same room with someone who wants you dead is not okay. Your fear is like Godiva chocolate to him or her. By nervously staying in the room, you allow him to scare and bully you—not a good power move.

The Go Public Policy

You can avoid being tempted by the Pollyanna Plan if you

have previously employed the Go Public Policy. It's simple. Blab to everyone you know—friends, co-workers (if they won't think you are nuts) and family. Invariably, killers are the nicest guys and many people, including the legal community, won't believe you. But enough people will such that:

• You are unlikely to be invited to the same events as X.

• In the improbable chance that you do intersect with X, those around you won't expect the Pollyanna Plan. They probably wouldn't mind if you screamed and ran.

If you pursue the Go Public Policy, be prepared for a bit of rejection. Some folks will take his side: the deluded ("but he's so humble and sweet"), the bought-off, the misogynists, and the superstitious who think death threats are infectious. You are better off without these people in your life anyway, unless one of them is your boss.

When you go public, X will know that you are aware of his intentions (in case he thought his plans were secret); this has more pros than cons. But seriously consider how far to go in the public realm: the written word in online social media or in printed media might bring a lawsuit your way and even worse, self-righteous wrath motivating him to defend his good name. Word of mouth is much safer. You want X to know you have people on your side who believe he is a threat. In the event of any harm to you, he is likely to be a suspect. Cold comfort, I know. But it is a handy deterrent because he needs more guts to do the deed. How foolhardy is he? How much of a coward? This brings us to the next imperative.

Know Your Predator

Like all prey, the more you know about your oppressor's mindset, the better you can protect yourself. For example, let's say X is a coward at heart, lazy, faints at the sight of blood and is afraid of jail. Unfortunately, he can afford to have someone else do his dirty work, but happily, he is a miser. A poor fellow, caught between the proverbial rock and hard place.

Most auspiciously, X may well consider you stupid and inept. If someone is audacious enough to consider killing, he or she must have a giant ego. You've probably had occasion to observe his efforts to stalk or intimidate. Even if these efforts have been feeble and easy to deflect, please remember, it takes only one slip up on your part for him to win; the odds are in his favor if he just keeps fishing. Regrettably, X probably feels superior to all other humans and has gotten away with various and sundry frauds. No doubt, he prides himself on cleverness and can easily talk himself into complete invincibility: bad news for you.

Any tyrant's interior landscape has its strengths and weaknesses. It's vital to keep your Security Plan polished and well-used.

The Bodyguard - Yes!

While you would love to employ a gorgeous hunk during the

times X is likely to show up, consider X's emotional traits. If he is a jealous type, as many intimidators are, it's better to hire a woman who looks like wallpaper. Act like she is your new best friend; he will think you are too clueless to hire a bodyguard. And remember, a female guard can follow you into the restroom.

If you must employ a man, use the dopey-looking overweight kind (armed to the teeth under his bulky clothing). I have just the guy for you. X won't think he is a date or a bodyguard. It is helpful to create an appropriate "job" for the man such as waiter, mover, photographer or ornithologist (those binoculars are handy) for an outdoor event.

If your budget tanks, take a sharp-eyed girlfriend with you who has orders to stick to you like sunburn at the beach. Her job is not jujitsu, but to be a witness, a priceless aid. Most killers prefer anonymity.

The Spiritual Solution

You might well ask, "What the heck kind of karma got you into this situation?" Death tends to bring up afterlife issues. Meet them head on. A death threat is a great kick in the rear to explore your personal beliefs about the sacred. Because—be honest—you don't know if you will have a tomorrow. Talk to spiritual people you can trust, from friends to psychics to the religiously ordained.

In New Age parlance, you may consider your death threat a

divine gift. You have been bequeathed with a continual flow of death consciousness in your everyday life. How best to use this honor in a positive way? Volunteer at your temple or church, hospital, homeless shelter, hospice or animal care facility.

If you consider New Age thinking a crock, you could simply pray a lot to God, Buddha, Allah or to Whom It May Concern. Even scientists say that prayer works. Agnostics and atheists might want to check out a Higher Power and get friendly with him/her/it. I found a boulder I can sit on that works well as a Higher Power; after all, it supports me, it is beautiful, has a great view and is unmovable.

To avoid excessive anger, bitterness and victim mentality within, consider establishing a relationship with your tormenter's higher self on the ethereal level since no relationship on the physical plane is possible. This type of solution must be within your belief system; you might surround him with gold light, or visualize him wearing angel wings or Mickey Mouse ears. Or, if you prefer, visualize X being sucked up by a giant vacuum cleaner, which is then emptied into outer space.

You can do all of the above as needed, and it will work for you in a messy but positive way, allowing you to continue moving through life with relative peace, considering.

Chapter 18
Sentence Interruptus

"If our raft had shot through those rapids on the right side instead of the left..." My old neighborhood friend let her sentence drift away into the ether as she normally did. As usual, I wanted to grill her about what happened next. Sometimes I probed Merry with possible sentence endings, trying to force some likely conclusion. But this became hard work when her habit was to fade out every sentence, leaving the listener hanging. With Merry, I had learned to avoid futility and instead, silently finish the sentence myself. If she had shot through the rapids on the right, she wouldn't have run into the bear who ate Tom's arm. Or, she wouldn't have dumped the Microsoft CEO in the drink. Or, she would have been thrown against sweet Jeremy rather than grumpy Scott.

An emergency room nurse who also ran a river rafting company, Merry always challenged herself with helping people

111

in their most dire traumas, including the swiftest rivers on Earth. Both jobs demanded quick decisive brain power and I admired her skills and ambition. But away from work, Merry dithered and I often thought that her opposite mental states – quick and sure versus vague and dreamy—seemed to create a balance in Merry's life. Maybe she ran out of decision-making neurons after a shift in the ER or after a few days guiding groups on a river. I couldn't fault her. My neurons would probably deplete after three minutes in either of those situations. I could understand if she got tired of rescuing people and needed to empty her mind for a while. Or perhaps she was addicted to danger; letting others end your sentences was certainly high-risk behavior. What if she said, "I think I'll walk to the bridge…" and someone added, "…and jump off."

But I found it interesting that Merry resembled her mother (I had known both for many years) in this unusual characteristic. Perhaps genes played a role. Except that her mom, Jill, always had a quirky smile waiting to break out and I knew she wanted me to finish her thoughts with a joke. When preparing a meal, Jill, a nervous cook, might say, "The pickles…"

"Perfect with the ice cream I brought," I'd quip. Corny, yes, but it helped us get a semblance of dinner on the table.

As I thought more about this strange phenomenon, I felt it deserved a name, Sentence Interruptus: people who started sentences but forgot to end them. There were more of these folks around than you would imagine. In times of stress or embarrassment, I reluctantly numbered myself among them.

I understood dithering as a socially acceptable female strategy, a way to give away personal power to others and allow them to make the decisions. To literally finish your sentences, create your world, and, in the bargain, consider you alluring and feminine.

But I didn't want to create Merry's realities for her. When I was with Merry, I indulged my inner preferences instead. If she said, "What if we cancel our picnic on Saturday..." I let my imagination run. Instead, I'll fly away in a hot air balloon through sunny skies. Or perhaps I'll go to the museum to see the Vampire exhibit, meet a cute and funny guy and we'll laugh all afternoon. Or maybe I'll scratch my pet cockatiel's ears for two hours and commune with him on an avian cosmic level. Thus, I transferred my annoyance at Merry's ambiguity into personal amusement.

Strangely, not long after this fantasy session, I met an attractive man one day at the art museum. His sweet, quiet ways blinded me to his grammar deficiencies. While we were in the getting-acquainted phase, I asked him questions about his life and he talked at length about himself. It took me awhile to realize that if I stopped asking questions about him, loud silences ensued. If I kept my mouth shut, he might ultimately insert an inquisitive, "So...?" And if I didn't fill the long blank space, he might add, "What do you...?" More quiet. If I waited for him to complete a question or sentence, our relationship would have been as soundless as outer space.

So now I had doubled the amount of Sentence Interruptus in my life. But I noticed that if I finished his phrase with words he didn't approve of, he was quick to correct me. This was Sentence Interruptus with a twist: he gave me the illusion of power by letting me proceed to a conclusion. But his quick corrections clued me in to his real agenda. I was supposed to second guess him. He expected me to be a psychic, to know what he wanted and supply it to him: a lazy masculine form of control in the guise of Sentence Interruptus.

One day when he arrived at my condo building's parking lot, I felt friendly and invited him upstairs to relax awhile. He responded to what I thought was a delectable offer with one word, "Fish..."

I was confused. Did something about my attempt at a sexy invitation remind him of fish? Did he want to buy seafood? "What do you have in mind?" I asked with an edge in my voice, not accustomed to being spurned for fish.

"Feed..." he said. Getting a verb out of him was a feat. As usual, I complied. He drove me to a 7-11 store and bought a loaf of soft white bread which he tossed in the back seat. Next, we headed to a long breakwater I had never seen before in Waikiki. It turned out to be fun strolling far out into the sea, as if we were walking on the surface with waves splashing at our ankles, feeding the abundant wildlife that leaped and snapped at our offerings.

When we returned to my condo, he had a headache. I thought that was supposed to be a woman's excuse. Over time, when I got too close, he might develop a sudden need to see a whale: "Whale..." he'd murmur (although he'd grown up in Hawaii, he'd never seen one). Or he would say, "Pirate..." And I would figure out that he wanted to visit a pirate ship—yes, Honolulu has one. One day, he had an urgent need for me to inspect his big toe for possible fungus. "Toe...green...?"

Unfortunately, I excelled at enabling, which I justified with the naïve belief that if I felt close to him, he would reciprocate. For me, to feel close meant successfully guessing what he wanted by interpreting his sparse words. I would ask, "Your toe is falling off?" "You don't like green?" And the verbal charades would proceed until he had corrected me (with the least number of words) into fulfilling his next intimacy prevention task. Although examining his adorable big toe did result in physical chumminess, it was a little more clinical than what I wanted with him. He kept pursuing me with several dates a week and prolonged sexy kisses now and then, just enough to keep me very interested.

I completed his sentences for several months, a month longer than I should have due to his pretty boy appeal.

Consider an inverse scale: his lack of verbal skills was in direct inverse proportion to the perfection of his high cheekbones, almond eyes and full lips. Even his feet with his fungus-free toes were lovely. I was a fool for male beauty. If he had added a sense of humor to the mix, he would have gotten still another month. I own my female weaknesses. But my Closeness is Reciprocal theory didn't work with him. Just because I wanted to bond didn't mean he wanted to or was able to.

Eventually I perceived his overall pattern of excuses and inadvertently found a source of inner satisfaction at last. Like an art collector, I began to amass a chronicle of his more creative emotional evasion efforts, and grew to admire them. He may hold the Guinness World record for Intimacy Avoidance. For example, there was the night he couldn't stay any longer because, as he said, "Centipedes..." I came to understand this was a killing spree at his home where he decapitated three-foot-long centipedes which gave him a major case of the willies. I could hardly blame him.

Another time, he said, "Vog..." A nearby volcano had blown sulphur dioxide on us which the locals called vog (rhymes with fog) and is as miserable as smog. After a lengthy guessing game, I learned he was terminally distracted by burning eyes and a queasy stomach. Not his fault, right? It was particularly curious that his reasons for avoiding me were always liberally laced with his innocence: a great technique that kept me coming back. What a master.

I discovered I had a real love of watching how far a person would pursue a strange habit. Furthermore, I had a perverse fascination for observing natural consequences: how far would he go before I'd had enough or before he hung himself? Needless to say, one day I realized, no matter how amazing his determination to avoid commitment, this prolonged distance had become detrimental to forming a lasting relationship and was a bit demeaning to me. I knew with a late-blooming inner certainty that I had no desire to plumb the depths of his psyche to see what lay beneath all his inventive pretexts, whether it be a mother complex or a simple need for Viagra.

I was just plain tired of emotional kindergarten: his aloofness, my second-guessing and being wrong most of the time. No more Ms. Nice Girl. I took a moral stand: the power-mongering type of Sentence Interruptus had no place in my life. Proud of my boundary-setting, I ate a tofu ice cream sundae to celebrate.

In the long run, I kept my feminine-style and giggly-style Sentence Interruptus friends around: they made me laugh and gave me time to bathe in my private mental world which I relished. I admit that at times, when Merry or Jill dithered, I was tempted to say, "Spit it out! What are you talking about?" But, realistically, I knew they wouldn't change their lifetime habits. And I loved them. So I let them falter and fade with a refreshing absence of a negative agenda, as compared to Mr. Silent Dominator. Merry, Jill and I didn't push each other. In due time, we always figured out what to do next; they with rested brain cells and perhaps feeling girly. As for me, I enjoyed abundant chuckles, both inner and outer.

Chapter 19
Riding Lessons

When I was a kid, I secretly named the neighbor's giant quarter horse, Death Wish. If Paint (his real name) had had his way, he would have ground me under his feet, or worse. At a recent reunion of the old neighborhood kids I grew up with, Paint's name came up. One of my aging friends, Nancy, had dream parents who let her keep a horse in their pasture and all were free to ride him in those innocent days before lawsuit fears and hovering parents. As our jolly reunion progressed, the wine flowed among them and permitted my own free-wheeling talk. Late in the evening, for the first time in fifty years, I felt free to reveal the horrors I had endured with Paint. When I was young, I imagined myself to be a natural cowgirl and never admitted to the deathly reality of my adventures on Paint. To keep up my competent and fearless Tough Girl position (which my parents expected of me) in our tight-knit community, my family and my inflated personality gave me no other choices. It took all these decades to pare my ego down to a manageable size and dare to speak the truth. Besides, I wanted to hear everyone else's hair-raising stories about Paint, so I would feel better about my cowardice.

Our cozy group of aged, former neighbors was delighted to reminisce, and remembered that Paint was a retired parade horse. Though I questioned whether he had the discipline necessary to work a parade route, Nancy insisted. To my surprise, my childhood buddies had fond memories of Paint. He was an enormous animal, a rich deep brown everywhere except for a white slash down his forehead that looked like a haphazard encounter with a paintbrush. I found him angry and barely trained. His dark eyes and flaring nostrils directed a bolt of cold fear that started at my throat and traveled all the way down to my wobbling knees. He terrified me with a delicious dread that kept me jittery, both anxious and eager to ride, wondering what dirty tricks he had in store that day. At the same time, Paint felt familiar, like life with Mom, her boyfriends, fiancés, husbands and my older sisters—wild and unpredictable. My job was to stay on Paint's back no matter what. As long as I stuck to him like a leech, my unspoken goal in life was simple and not unlike the objective within my family: to survive. I never breached my sacred silence about this desperate quest, probably because I was so caught up in my phony bravado I remained unconscious of this imperative. But it underlay my every waking moment between the ages of nine to fourteen. Can something as ephemeral as a self-image, an illusion, kill you? If Paint could talk, his answer would have been a resounding "Yes," along with a whinnying snicker.

Everyone rode Paint bareback; no one in the neighborhood could afford a saddle. When I jumped on Paint's back and trotted off one day, in a typical maneuver, he abruptly whirled in a hard left off of the sandy abandoned inter-urban rail line we usually rode. When his spin didn't unseat me, all at once he charged into the nearby, dense forest at a hard gallop, a rare ploy on his part. I held on tight, pressing my legs like steel clamps around his wide girth while I yanked back on the reins. Paint far outranked me in both muscle power and temper.

As he sped toward a huge tree, I twined one hand around his mane and with the other I pulled on the reins, which didn't cause him to even blink, let alone slow down. When we neared the tree, I crouched low and I spied the thick, low-slung branch Paint probably saw, too, and was likely planning to use for my decapitation. Streamlined into the almost horizontal slant of his neck like an Indian, I was one with creation's pulsing power, ready when, at the last second, the horse cleverly swerved from impact with the tree trunk and skimmed under the branch. Once he realized that I still clung to him, he galloped on, but seemed to lack further ideas for dumping me. Two death threats a day were apparently his maximum.

When he slowed to a lope, I returned him to the inter-urban path and we cantered to my neighbors in the field. It seemed to me, Paint invested more of his energy trying to get rid of me than he would have spent on a pleasant half-hour ride; very similar to some boyfriends I would have in the future. Back in the pasture, I told my friends what a fun jaunt we had, leaving out the trees, branches, panic and near-death. But, as per normal with a ride on Paint, my stomach shook for the rest of the day.

It was important to keep up my expected cowgirl image. "Grin and bear it" was our family motto. Complaining was for wimps and not allowed in our household. This was influenced by Dad's former Marine ethos and long-lasting Secret Service job, along with Mom's pioneer parents, all of whom had Depression-era resilience tossed into the mix for good measure. Riding was supposed to be fun, the dream of every little girl, and I was Ms. Rough Rider. Who was I to go against all of these instilled group ideals I had to live up to?

I could count on Paint to prepare exciting new agendas for me. When I had free time from school or chores, I raced to the pasture, my nerves jangling as wildly as a leaf in a windstorm. Although none of the neighborhood parents made any rules concerning Paint, I only rode when Nancy was home and said, "Sure, go ahead." When she did, I talked to Paint quietly, reviewing what he had done wrong the week before. I told him to give me a nice ride. But Paint had endless creative ideas. One day, much to my surprise, he refused to leave the pasture. When I kicked him to go, he splayed all four legs, dropped his head, and shot his back legs out. He bucked again and again while I held on for my precious life. I felt like a ball popping up and down inside a child's toy vacuum cleaner, my bones clacking with each bounce.

"Jerk his head up," Nancy yelled. I yanked up on the reins and by the umpteenth try, Paint raised his eyes, probably to see if I was still there rather than to obey. Shaking his head and snorting, Paint walked a few steps, as if complying with my kicks. But in an instant, I felt like I was on a swooping roller coaster hurtling downward; the bottom dropped out of my world. With a quick reflex, I leaped clear. It was a good move because in the next second I would have been crushed under a half-ton of horseflesh. Paint had suddenly folded his legs, dropped to the earth and rolled, hooves flailing high in the air, hoping to squash me, since he couldn't buck me off. With Paint (as with my mother), you never knew what would strike next, and it was usually catastrophic. With him, a death roll, buck or low tree limb; with Mom, new fiancés, booze or husbands.

When I confided all the ways Paint had tried to kill and maim me, my venerable companions seemed truly stunned. I expected to hear their tales of mayhem aboard his back, but they had happy memories of the old boy. I finally resorted to boldly asking, "Didn't that rascal horse do things like that to any of you guys?" The worst that had happened to one neighbor, Lani, was that Paint had given her a couple of small bucks. She had lost her seat, landed in the grass in front of her friends, and was mortified, wisely walking him calmly home afterwards.

Perhaps that was the difference. Whatever Paint did to me, I jumped back on him with stereotypical self-improvement refrains in my mind: "Always get back on the horse/car/rollercoaster/bicycle right away, or else you'll be afraid forever." I remounted this troublesome equine every time and my stomach never lowered from its Paint position in my throat. Riding Paint did not conquer fear, it increased the shakes exponentially. But I would never admit it; my family's survivalist beliefs always rode Paint along with me.

Another potent homily was: "Face your fears or else they will rule your subconscious." With Paint, fear totally ruled my subconscious. But I got better and better at pretending it didn't.

An even more important lesson seeped into me: "Never tell others when you are terrified or when someone wants to kill you." I don't remember anyone giving me specific instructions on how to live an exemplary life, but I deeply absorbed this message, regardless of origin. After all, it took me more than fifty years to confide my Paint-inspired panic to my childhood

124

comrades and just about that long to tell therapists about other horrors in my life: Mom's second husband's psychotic breakdown; her various boyfriends chasing and kissing me; and when I came of age, my own boyfriends beating me and/or making a plan to murder me.

Late in adulthood, my oldest sister thought to tell me that my Secret Service agent father (who died when I was eight) had always counseled her to "Stay out of the line of fire." That advice could have helped me with Paint, stepfathers and boyfriends (both Mom's and mine). But it came a bit late for me.

It shook me up that Paint had not tried to decapitate any of my neighbors. Apparently I was the only one to suffer extensive horse-abuse. Lani had experienced a minor scrape with Paint. And Lani had married two wife-beaters. All of us timeworn friends had quietly sighed with relief when the first husband's lungs gave out after thirty years of Lani's black eyes. "Free at last," we collectively thought. But she promptly found wife-beater #2 who luckily, grew elderly and lacked enough strength to hurt her much, for which we were all thankful.

Could there be a link between abusive horses and violent men? My cynical (and probably accurate) side had learned that predators, animal and human, can sense a milquetoast and take immediate advantage. I had a worse track record with Paint than Lani, a sobering insight indeed. I had always felt sorry for

Lani, but never for myself. Such clearheaded thoughts made me wonder for the first time why I had inevitably returned for more abuse from Paint (and the various men). A kid doesn't have much choice about her stepfathers or her Mom's male companions, but, as for my boyfriends, I could have simply accepted that they didn't like me or enjoyed walloping me way too much and walked away. Ah, the glory of options, which I now realize I have spread before me like a nourishing buffet.

Now that I have come clean and admitted to Paint's evil dominion and that of several men, it's time to offer myself some sympathy, give myself a round of applause to celebrate survival and to absorb the meaning and the joys of "Adios." Note for the future: Stay out of the line of fire.

Medicine Wheel South
The Unknown Hawaii

On the traditional Native American medicine wheel, the South represents the physical world, a place of growth and manifestation; an apt symbol for the child and for innocence. Nurturing, family, integrity, truth and hard work belong in the South.

In this collection of humorous stories, I write about Hawaii, where I have spent much of my time for the last twenty years. With the most recently formed real estate on earth and a daily erupting volcano creating ever more land, Hawaii lends itself to themes of phantasmagoric regeneration and ultimate creativity grounded in ever new physical space. Besides, Hawaii's reputation as a paradise on earth is too rich a target to ignore.

Chapter 21
Ms. Sears Wall

"Buildings crash around me. Damn. My ears ache," Ms. Wall sobbed as bulldozers ripped through the concrete around her.

"Ms. Wall, do I hear the usual complaining and weeping from you?" asked the female giant Columbia, a forty-foot statue erected in the 1800s from her lofty perch on the hillside overlooking the Kakaako district of Honolulu (before the Statue of Liberty became the symbol for America, Columbia was the name for the great American continent). She could see ten giant cranes working on building sites throughout the area. But, at her quiet feet, the dead slept in Punchbowl Military Cemetery.

"Oh, you're so serene and detached up there looking after your families in the big burial ground. You have no idea what we go through down here, risking our lives to hold up these

129

buildings for decades. And then, one day, smash, they grind us into bits with no appreciation for all we've done." Ms. Wall lifted a jagged concrete fist, with a long rebar finger sticking out, toward Columbia.

"Ms. Sears Wall, I did appreciate you. Did you know that I would sneak out past the guards at night to go to Sears' evening sales? I got great bargains. I love to dress up in the dark when no one can see me. In the morning, I stow my wardrobe in a hole beneath my base and resume my daily monochrome severity. People like to see me being serious, holding my arms outstretched toward them to comfort them in their mourning. But I spent much of my precious night life with you, dear Ms. Wall.

"But now, I'm sorry to tell you, it is time to face your noisy reality; you must return to dust for a while. It happens to all of us. I should know, what with my work here at the graveyard. You are the women's clothes specialist and I am the expert in corporal transitions. You will be calmer if I explain the process you can expect. Unfortunately that nasty steam shovel will knock you down. But that's far from the end. You'll come stay with me awhile and have a nice rest and think about what kind of wall you might want to be next time around. How about a wall in a family home?"

"Oh, it's easy for you to say," Ms. Sears Wall said. "No one is turning you into tiny particles. Oh no, that giant excavator is coming closer and closer. He's going to get me any minute!" Sears Wall cried, fat drops of moisture rolling down her mildewed green sides.

"Oh, I am sorry it's coming so fast now, dear," Columbia said. "The moment we completely collapse can be difficult. Remember your meditation lessons, Sears? Breathe deeply with me. One in, one out. Two in, two out. Focus on your third eye, your spiritual essence and it will all come naturally to you," Columbia wisely counseled. "Getting knocked over will be a short shock, then your endorphins will carry you away from pain. Be brave. I know you can do it with ease and grace."

"Arrrgh. Ouch. Ohhhhh, I'm falling down, down, down," Sears gurgled, her voice slowly fading away.

Columbia watched her crumple into cement pieces while a great cloud of sandy powder arose and lifted high into the air, Ms. Sears Wall's spirit going into Wall heaven. "There you go, my lovely Sears. See, was that so bad?"

Ms. Sears Wall floated up, caught a breeze and wafted over to Columbia up on her hill. "It was horrible," Sears wailed. "Meditation didn't work." She paused and drifted on the breeze. "Well, it helped a little. Then my ashy cloud lifted out of the rubble and I didn't feel the pain of my concrete blocks lying wrecked all over the place. But I don't want to go through that again."

"Of course, you don't, my sweet Sears. Take all the time you want to think about what kind of wall you would like to be next. All your dust and concrete blocks will be recycled into new cement. Would you like to be a wall in a spa and listen to New Age music?"

Sears choked. "Oh, lord, no! I want more action than that; remember, I already spent decades watching women try on clothes all day, although I saw a lot of interesting bodies. And I slanted the mirrors a little bit back to slenderize them; I could tell they liked that. But I'm ready for some real excitement now. Perhaps I'll be a wall at a stadium so I can watch football games and listen to rock concerts."

"Bless you, my child," said Columbia. "It will be the best of both worlds for you, combining great excitement and joy with quiet times between events. And you'll be outdoors enjoying all of nature's seasons. I'll put in a good word for you with the God of Walls."

Chapter 22
Growing Feet in Hawaii

In my son's grade school in Hawaii, shoes were not required. Most kids went barefoot, leaving their dusty, splayed toes looking childishly free. And at home in Hawaii, all footwear is left outside the door. We slap around barefoot inside. On sport's teams, kids wear athletic shoes, but quickly kick them off when the game is over.

Around town, going to a movie or shopping, we wear the state's standard footwear, flip-flops, locally called "slippahs" (pigeon for slippers). In junior and senior high school, these are the default "shoe," handy for the beach and for quickly slipping off at home and at friends' houses. By eighth grade, my son's large puppy feet had morphed to a size twelve. A kind foot god heard my mother prayers to slow the growth to an ultimate size thirteen by high school.

My son spent five years in college on the mainland and

learned foreign footwear habits. But each time he returned home for holidays, he reverted to Hawaii customs, so I didn't see any difference in his feet until he began to think about job interviews. With his two degrees in business, and many years spent using his head, I should have been prepared for a big change at the other end of his body.

Wing-tips were a source of hippy distain and ridicule in the 1960s when I came of age. They were a symbol for the worst excesses of the business world establishment and the military/industrial complex, all of which were our enemies at the time. Over the Christmas holidays, when my son declared wing-tips all the rage in the business world, I snorted with laughter. The universe had cycled around with a just comeuppance. But besotted mother devotion resulted in a trip to the mall. Heads together, we analyzed differing brands, colors and styles of wing-tips; I bought him his favorite pair.

While at the Nordstrom's shoe smorgasbord, I received further lessons in men's stylish feet. A young man about town, either in Hawaii or on the mainland, must also have the proper moccasin-style shoe that can be worn without socks and easily slipped off at a friend's doorstep in Hawaii. We were at the December 26 sales, so we added a pair of discounted Sperry's. After all, he was my only begotten son.

Next, I learned subtleties about male foot fashion. Informal footwear had two levels: the moccasin spin-off (one step above flip-flops) and an upper level casual for going on a date or to a nice club. For this, modified wing-tips with some suede (all suede being slightly sleazy) fit the bill.

Mother love only went so far, even at post-Christmas sales. My emotional limit was breached with one pair of wing-tips. My son sprang for wing-tips number two.

Thus, we arrived home with three new pairs of shoes for my son's dawning era in his life-to-be as a gainfully employed man. Although he had graduated from college, for me, his real rite of passage took place that day after Christmas when his feet grew up.

Chapter 23
Light Plants

The old water supply pumping station is made of red brick with a high tower that seems to stand guard over the building's large arches that resemble lines of inquisitive eyebrows on every side. Wandering on the beach one day, I see the old abandoned building a couple of blocks from the shore. An odd tickling sensation in my stomach seems to pull me forward and I grin. Why not? I walk over. No one else is around as the sun sinks toward the horizon. Broken glass crunches underfoot and gusty trade winds blow palm tree fronds horizontal. The giant tree leaves alternately droop or bounce in the temperamental breezes as if afflicted with arboreal bipolar disorder. Why is this building abandoned, with its fanciful architecture from the last century? It could be a delightful museum or atmospheric old-world-style restaurant. Better yet, it looks like it could be a home to a family of gnomes, or maybe even ogres. I see a scraping door, waving me toward it in the fitful winds. I can't resist.

I enter and brush soft cobwebs away from interior doorways. Enough orange light from the lowered sun floods the large arched windows for me to clearly see my way around and enjoy a sherbet glow. I could imagine I had stepped into a rusty Disney Magic Castle. I shuffle through clanking metal and glass rubble and explore every corner of the brick interior rooms; in the back are small former offices or bedrooms. I spy no tiny or ugly creatures. A stairway curves up and I follow it to a long balcony with more rooms running along it. One room pulls me in; its curved shape echoes the arc of the staircase. In the far corner of this smile-shaped room, I walk toward what looks like a long closet with a door hanging askew.

I pull the squeaking door open and enter a musty black space, my eyes adjusting to the dim. The enfolding velvet darkness pulls me like a magnetic force, gently attracting me. Once again, my stomach contracts as if fingers tickle it and I giggle, letting myself be drawn forward. As my eyes slowly adjust, I notice spiral shapes that are slightly illumined. I search for light from a high window, but see no source for the clarity of these forms. Some are as high as my head, others diminished to a toylike size. A few shapes glow with a greenish color, others are more blueish. One is a pink hue. I reach my hand out waist-high to touch the golden one nearest to me. When I touch it, will I feel a vibration, or an electric warmth, or more tickles? All at once, I hear a loud "crack." I jump in alarm, wondering if I've been electrocuted, even though I haven't touched the glowing forms yet. But maybe my thoughts or intentions set something off. At least, I know my guilty conscience is alive and well. I wiggle my arm and it's fine. I peer around; the lights serenely glow unfazed by the noise or my alarm. Then I realize that a gust of wind must have slammed the front door shut. I rush down the stairs in the fading light. Just as I thought, the door is clamped tight. I tug, to no avail. I kick the door, hoping to loosen it. But it is locked. I slump down to the floor. What can I do? No one will hear me in this isolated spot. I feel my heart thud in my chest. I raise my knees and rest my head on them, eyes closed. I will have to spend the night here. I remember a friend, a policeman who was called to resolve a noise in an abandoned building. Once inside, he chased a stray dog out and somehow the entry door slammed and locked him in. Mortified, he had to call in for back-up to release him. By contrast, I am lucky to be a simpleton on my own who can hide my ordeal; no one else need ever know. On the other hand, I am stuck.

By the time I raise my head, the sun has disappeared and I am in inky blackness on this moonless night. As I peer around, I feel one impulse: I must return to the closet upstairs that, for some reason, holds soft lights and a secure feeling. But a suspicious little gremlin flares in my mind. What if those ethereal illuminations are a trap? They might intend evil, luring me by friendly tickles. But they are my only source of light. Stumbling through glass shards and trash, I try to remember the route to the stairs. With arms outstretched like a blind person, I feel my way. Sometimes, I trip over debris or knock my face on a wall. At last I feel the curved bannister of the stairs. Now I inch my way to the room with the rounded walls and the special closet.

I grope across the floor and find the closet door hanging at an angle. For a moment, I pause to wipe my hands, stringy with cobwebs (old ones vacated by spiders I hope), on my shorts. When I enter the closet, I see the softly glowing spirals. How can such an old wrecked closet feel like home? Surely, if there were evil here, I would feel it. But I remember thinking the same thing about a boyfriend or two, and being proved terribly wrong. Regardless, as I gaze at the field of colors, I feel compelled to walk forward to be among them, until they surround me on all sides, a subtle array in every size, some towering above my head. The closet expands so far, I can't see where it ends and I am in a forest of friendly sculptures, some old growth, some young and sprightly, nearly bouncing with energy. Reaching out, I touch a lavender spiral, just my height, and I feel a gentle tingling down my arm and into my chest. I sigh with contentment.

With nothing else to do, I examine the shining spiral shapes that look like giant coiled fern fronds just being born as they uncurl into the light. I notice that the frond-like shapes are segmented into pieces about two inches long. I stroke the lavender "light-plant" as I am beginning to think of it, feeling the tiny joints. As I massage the shapes, suddenly a fragment breaks off in my hand. I jerk my body backwards, "Oh, no," I say, afraid some kind of plant blood or sap will spurt out. But the piece of light in my hand continues to glow and the light-plant appears calm and vital as ever.

In fact, I seem to hear a voice in my mind, "Hey, it's nice to see someone in this old place. Because we like you, you can take as many pieces as you need. Silently speak to the fragment in your hand, requesting the amount of light you need. Try it."

"Okay," I say, hesitating. "But aren't I taking advantage of you?"

"I wouldn't offer if I didn't mean it." The light-plant sways as if in a breeze.

I look at the piece of lavender in my hand, and feeling foolish, I aim a thought at it: "Please become as bright as a flashlight so I can walk around this old building." Whoosh! The lavender light is suddenly intense. "Wow!"

All at once, I am greedy for an even brighter setting. I ask, "Are you sure it's all right to use more pieces?"

"Absolutely. Have fun. But here's the deal. We've rigged it

so only those people who are pure of heart can see these lights. And we get to define 'pure of heart'."

I'm so dazzled by the fairyland and my control over it, I don't stop to think beyond that. I pluck every color I can find and, as I do, I realize I have a plan of escape in my hands. "Light-plant, are there others in town who can see these lights?"

"A few." The lavender light seems to giggle by flashing undulating ribbons of sparkles around the room.

It's worth a chance to try. Using the odd lanterns to illuminate my path around the building, I amp up the pieces to a shining brilliance and find spots in the building to place them: balanced on door knobs, along railings and the tops of counters, shelves and on the rims of open doors. Soon the whole building blazes as if lit up for a grand party. The arched windows look elegant and the old tower casts stately shadows. I make my way downstairs, placing lights all around, smiling at their festive air, for I expect horse-drawn carriages to pull up with women dressed in silky ball gowns on the arms of men in formal black tie.

Instead I see headlights and immediately order all the lights to douse themselves. Even though I long for rescue, I feel protective of these sweet glowing beings and don't want our secret discovered. The car lights bounce along the uneven dirt road approaching the abandoned building and I hold my breath, hoping the car does not contain people coming to the remote place to party or deal drugs. When I see the logo of a security firm on the car door, I release a long breath. Whew.

I stumble in the sudden darkness to a cracked window and wave. "Help, I'm locked in here," I call. The security guard shines his LED light on me. Its harsh glare hurts my eyes, unlike the serene glow from my light-plants.

The guard unlocks the door, and I see a large Polynesian, probably Samoan or Fijian, with tattoos spiraling up his arms. I pray that he is worthy, as the lights told me. With a brusque voice, he questions me as if to determine whether I'm stoned or nuts. When my panicky answers seem to convince him I am a harmless fool, his eyes relax and he offers me a ride to my car at the beach parking lot. As I thank him, I ask him if the old building is a regular part of his route each night.

"Oh, heck, no. This is way outside my jurisdiction. It must have been my imagination, but I thought I saw lights out here." He shakes his head. "But it couldn't have been. You don't even have a flashlight."

As I slump, relaxed in the front seat, I smile to myself, thinking about the next time I visit the magic plants. I have a lot of questions to ask them. Where did you come from? How do you talk to me? What is the source of your light? Can you read the future and help me solve all my problems? Is my current boyfriend worth keeping around? Should I invest in

Alibaba?

The next evening I park my car a block away and trot into the building and up to the arched room, my mind filled with all my questions. But the room is empty; the enchanted plants have disappeared. Tears spring to my eyes, I am so disappointed. But I remember their magical light and their help, saving me from a cold and possibly dangerous night in the abandoned building. Instead of my greedy curiosity, wanting to know more, desiring to grasp advantages, I decide to relish their beauty and their gift as a memory.

Chapter 24
Frozen Boulders

"Climb every mountain, ford every stream, follow every rainbow…" Keala's strong clear voice pierced the bright sunlit day as we struggled up a steep slope above the tree line of Mauna Kea on the Big Island of Hawaii. Her white hair reflected the sun, almost as if she herself was a beam of light. Her muscular, wiry legs never tired.

"Pipe down with the Broadway tunes, Keala," I hollered as I sagged against a boulder to catch my breath. I loved my dear friend, but I also craved quiet on this, the holiest mountain in all of Polynesia. Ever since I had set foot on the enormous volcanic cinder cone, I had felt like I had come home. In spite of the twenty-five pound backpack I carried, my footsteps felt lighter than normal. I wished I had colossal arms that could hug the whole mountain. I wanted to continue walking around it for the rest of my life, with a water break every hour, however. We had been trekking for the past two hours and I was ready for a pause.

"…'til you fiiind your dreeeam," Keala warbled with operatic exaggeration, her arms swinging wide to include our stunning view of the turquoise Pacific below us.

"My dream is to sleep on this cozy rock." I snuggled into the indented curve in the lava, just right for my tired body. "What a pest," I muttered, annoyed at Keala's unending vibrant energy and noise on the trail. Just because her name meant "the pathway" in Hawaiian didn't make her Queen of the Hike.

Keala sat on the other side of the path; the last I saw, she was drawing designs in the dirt with a stick. I vaguely heard her murmur, "Well, I'll be darned. These ants are building the Parthenon." On our last hike, her ants had built the Lighthouse at Alexandria. Keala saw the best ants.

It seemed like two minutes later when Keala spoke low in my ear. "Cate, did you see that field of boulders?"

"Of course I did," I said as I sleepily waved my arm in the general direction of the many acres of angled highland terrain on our right-hand side.

"But, did you see them?"

I have a button in my brain labeled "What Keala Sees." I know when I push that button, something spectacular will arise. I shrugged myself awake, clicked my mental button and looked again at the adjacent steep mountain slope, randomly strewn with chunks of old lava, some bigger than a truck. They were stationery, just like me at this moment, taking a break in life's ongoing trajectory to rest on the trail just as I was doing.

Each cast a clear shadow, as simple as the Zen rock gardens I had seen in Japan. Within each stone, more shadows showed knobs and curves, as if a giant had cast them in a sculpture studio to depict distinct personalities. As I gazed, the indentations in a rust-colored lava rock were perfectly placed to create large eyes, a tiny nose and a wide laughing mouth, all angled upward as if in communication with someone in the sky. Another black rock sported large bumps and craters that looked like slanted, downcast eyes, a protruding rodent-shaped nose and a frowning mouth like a gargoyle whose job was to protect the territory. Why did I see a face in almost every stone? We seemed like an "ohana," a makeshift family. Or perhaps I was desperate for company other than Keala.

We were all resting, but as I looked harder at them, I saw rocks of all sizes and shapes, in shades of gray, rust and black, each perched at a different angle on the slope, frozen in a suspended moment, caught in the act of tumbling down the mountainside. Just as I relaxed on the trail, the boulders seemed to wait for their journey to continue.

With sudden clarity, I saw that the rocks and I were the same, separated only by a different time scale. We had all been thrust into the world with volcanic force, landing wherever fate allowed. And suddenly we shared the same spot on a sacred mountainside. We waited for the next earthquake, storm or freezing/heating extreme that would unseat us and send us further on our path, I in human time and they in interminable time. But we were all impelled toward movement by outside forces. I was a sister to these rocks. I slowed to their rhythm and felt a satisfied peace to be sitting among them. A deep archaic part of me felt a kinship and a unity as we shared this mysterious journey.

When I glanced up, I wasn't surprised to hear Keala belting out an old rock 'n roll song; I saw her dancing on the path about twenty feet in front of me. Although ten years older than me (and I had just retired) her hips jutted and swayed like a teenager while her arms pivoted to the familiar refrain:

1, 2, 3 o'clock, 4 o'clock rock

5, 6, 7 o'clock, 8 o'clock rock

9, 10, 11 o'clock, 12 o'clock rock

We're gonna rock around the clock tonight.

"Yeah, I get it, Keala. We're in it together with these rocks, but right now, I'd rather hang out in geologic time for a while." Keala danced away while I closed my eyes and felt the solid stone hold my weight with ease.

Later, I continued walking, Keala barely visible in the distance. I veered off the path to visit this stone or the other, patting, leaning my full length against one, feeling the sun's captured heat, wondering and humming an old song. I was getting to be as bad as my old friend.

How does it feel
To be on your own
With no direction home
Like a complete unknown
Like a rolling stone?

For this field of boulders, home was a mountainside, where they nestled into earth between travels. But how far, when, and how quickly would they reach stasis? What was the goal? None of us would ever know. The rocks surrendered to nature's forces just as I did. And they submitted with grace and beauty, as I hoped to. How does it feel? Like an old stone, peaceful and vibrant. The boulders held happy or wrathful countenances, as varied as human moods.

I watched Keala's distant dance which almost looked like a high five from where I stood. I sent her a raised palm back. "Thank you for the Zen moments," I hollered into the clear mountain air. "And mahalo for being an amazing friend," I added.

Chapter 25
Dumpster Eyes

Outside my window, a thick tropical downpour fell, but my muscles twitched as usual for their daily walk. Several blocks away, a large recycling bin stood in the local high school parking lot, a perfect excuse for a rainy day walk. I grabbed my biggest umbrella and three tote bags filled with empty bottles, cans, papers and cardboard.

Dodging puddles, I zigzagged the few blocks with rainwater streaming off my umbrella. I enjoyed crisp air on my cheeks, which was unusual for Hawaii. I stopped near the recycling area where muddy water surrounded dented metal containers creating what looked like a small chocolate sea. Gingerly, I stepped up on a large piece of concrete, about one and one-half feet high, where I could reach the narrow three-foot window-like opening. The big receptacle had been painted white years ago; now chipped and peeling paint revealed red and green strips below the grimy white. In the first dark hole, I tossed my glass and plastic items and edged over to the center cavity for papers.

I leaned forward, noticing that sheets of cardboard filled about half the space. Then, unbelieving, I saw a pair of eyes staring at me from the dark depths. I pulled my hand back and teetered on the edge of the concrete. The cardboard had come alive! Once I regained my balance, I peered into the pit again and saw two more pairs of eyes—the small brown eyes of young teenaged boys.

I wondered what the proper etiquette was for encountering boys in a dumpster. They seemed uncertain, too. Should I be a stern adult and shoo them off? I was tempted to run away, forget I saw them and return with my trash another day. But maybe a joke would be best.

A sense of the absurd took over. I would treat them as if I was a visitor to their rusty home.

"Hi. How are you guys?" I asked.

"Okay," came a cautious reply.

"Can I throw some stuff in here?"

"Yeah." A friendly response came from the boy in the center of the bin, his eyes twinkling in the dim interior.

"Umm…where?" I didn't know how many kids were in there.

"That way." With a straight face, the boy pointed to a corner hidden from my view.

"Okay," I said as I tossed a few large pieces of cardboard where he had pointed.

"Hey," a voice protested from the corner while the three other boys erupted in hoots and guffaws.

I also laughed at the joke they had played on me and their companion. "Whoa, I'll throw the rest of the things that direction," I said pointing to a clear spot. "Watch out!"

To pitch my debris, I had to put down my umbrella and I was soon soaked. I looked at the boys nestled in cardboard and paper, in a cozy human-sized nest. "It looks dry and warm in there," I said after I tossed the last bit of paper in.

"Yeah," the leader said. "It's cool."

"It sure is. Bye-bye," I said. "Stay dry."

I sloshed away with a big smile between the rivulets running down my face. I stomped in every mud puddle in my path, just to enjoy the big splash. I remembered my childhood forts of days gone by, but none were as dry and strong as the recycling dumpster the young boys had discovered. Smart kids.

Chapter 26
Junkyard Radio

On my daily walks in Kakaako, an industrial coastal area of Honolulu currently undergoing gentrification, I can wander from a new condo building housing a TV station to a crammed appliance repair cubbyhole to various imaginative homeless shelters made out of overlapping tarps all in one block. One cool fall day (in Honolulu, that means 75 degrees), I took a new route down a crooked, narrow, one lane road. It wound past an auto repair shop and a lumber yard toward an old water pumping station, that had been abandoned for many years. Just past the pumping station, I suddenly came upon an odd log cabin I had never seen before in front of a large junkyard filled with crushed and twisted car parts, and stacks of computer and other machine fragments. The log cabin was decorated with a polished six-cylinder exhaust manifold resembling a shiny candleholder for six candles. Next to it, an antique tin Coke sign was nailed into the wall.

As I stared, a wrinkled brown face popped out of a window. "What are you doing here?" He frowned as his hoarse voice spat out the question.

"I love looking at all these marvelous shapes; they are like sculptures," I said as I drew back a step.

He slammed his window shut and disappeared inside. *I guess that's the last of him*, I thought.

I walked up to the chain link fence that hemmed the junkyard and pressed my nose through the diamond shaped opening; each eye had its own diamond and a full view of the massive piles of metal trash. A creaking and a wailing sound began from within the yard, and I searched for the source. Wrinkling my brow, I couldn't find where the sound came from.

When I heard a door slam near me, I jumped and looked around.

"Okay, c'mon in. Just be careful not to step on anything. They're sensitive." The small wiry man walked over to a door in the chain link fence and motioned me in.

"Who's sensitive?" I asked, confused.

He walked in and left the wire door hanging open while he strode on between huge piles of warped metal pieces. I skittered after him and was alarmed when the door clicked shut behind me.

"Where are you?" I called. All I heard was the squeaking and screeching sound, now louder. I followed where I thought he had gone and found myself in a valley surrounded by hills of old car parts.

By now the odd sound was closer and clear enough that I heard raspy words. "Who are you? Why are you here?"

The old man poked his brown face out from behind a carburetor. Soft white hair fell forward onto his brow. "God knows why, but they like you. They only talk to people they like."

"Who's 'they'? Are you some kind of ventriloquist? This is too weird," I said, looking around.

"Well, see that old radio near the top of the heap? It likes to talk a lot; old habit, I guess."

I looked up and saw a glint of blue light and a radio dial.

"Well, answer it," the man demanded. "It's not polite to stand there with your mouth open."

"I'm Cate," I called. "I came to visit because I love how you look."

"How could you?" the radio replied with a sob. "We come from disemboweled old cars and machines, the rejected innards no one wants."

"But I think you're beautiful. And if I think so, others will too," I reasoned.

With a flick of his head, the junkyard owner flipped his

white hair off his brow. "Unless you're crazy," he said thoughtfully.

"I'm not. But I am an artist," I said. "Well, some people think artists are nutty. But, at least, there are lots of artists who will find you lovely and fascinating. How would you like to become part of sculpture?"

"Can I still talk?" the radio asked.

"Sure, artists make talking sculptures all the time," I said. "I'll tell the whole Art Department at the University about you and lots of them will want you."

The proprietor shook his head. "But I have to meet every artist and art student and make sure they will be good to my precious junk."

"Sure, I understand; that makes perfect sense."

"But," the radio cried, "the artists can't use all of us. What will happen to the pieces not chosen?"

"I'll inform the photographers and the painters about you and they will immortalize you in paint and photos," I said with excitement, for I could almost see the compositions the artists would create.

The aged man put up his hand. "This is all well and good, but some of you will have to accept that it may be time for you to be recycled. This is the reality we all must face."

"No," the radio howled, "I want to be immortalized for eternity. Now."

"Look, Radio," the man said sternly, "you were going to be recycled anyway, so stop your whining. Now you have a chance at something else. That's life. Besides, recycling isn't the end of the world. In fact, it's how the world keeps itself going. I will be reprocessed someday. Even Ms. Fancy Artist here will be. So quit spouting off."

"Well, Mr. Wise Old Owl, I'll blather as much as I want because that's what I do and that's what you would do, too, if you were a radio. I was in a Mercedes, I might add, so I'm not your common *hoi polloi.*"

The old man glanced at me. "Just another day in the junkyard," he said with a grin.

Chapter 27
Teen Angels

Letter to the Editor
Honolulu TIMES

Dear Editor,

Today I must express my thanks to the two teenaged boy-angels who went with me on my walk. As you know, here in Hawaii, we are blessed with the Hawaiian *Awaiku*, special beings of light who help us every day. And personally, I don't think that enough of you in the wider public take full advantage of all they have to offer: protection, divine inspiration, healing, a belly laugh and just good company. Regardless, I have always seen the *Awaiku* as large *tutus* (grandmothers) with their colorful flowered muumuus swaying in the trade winds, playing their ukuleles.

It makes sense that the *Awaiku* would be equal opportunity

angels. Today, I made a point of asking for teenaged boy *Awaikus* to walk with me. The two young men were tall and muscular, like most Hawaiians, with black curly hair and skin the color of rich koa wood. And you wouldn't believe what they showed me: a jagged, cut-away cross section one hundred feet long of a huge Ala Moana shopping center parking lot. You can hardly imagine that hundreds of cars can sit on this thin layer made of concrete and rebar only eight inches thick!

Next, they showed me strong sparkling reflections of morning light under a concrete bridge. Who would think to look there? And near the bridge, a large male crested crane, majestic with blue feathers and imposing crown, stood fishing. He stared at me from three feet away as I crouched under the bridge. I gazed back and told him how beautiful he was.

Of course, those boy *Awaikus* also showed me more wahine in bikinis than I had ever noticed before. But, boys will be boys.

When we got to the ocean shore, we stopped, spellbound, to watch the acrobats atop those waves. I could feel my boy angels aching to be on their own surfboards on the large South Swell we get in the summer. I was happy to watch and not be seasick on the heaving seas. The boys laughed at me for being a wimp, and I said, "Hey, it's not always so easy to be in this body." And then my youths gave me a gift.

Usually I dump my anxieties in the great healing field of the ocean; I figure the sharks can get good use from them. But today the young men turned serious, one of them saying, "Great healing ocean, fill Cate with your strong energies of healing light." I felt a surge of ocean joy, like waves flowing through me. Thank you, men!

We walked back home together, I for one with a lighter step. They had one more gift for me. "Remember that dark-skinned teenager who held you up at gun-point thirty years ago?" one asked me. I gulped. How could I could ever forget that? Alone in the downtown tutoring center where I worked the night shift, I had stared down the barrel of that gun, barely seeing the thirteen-year-old boy and his group of friends. I had figured I was already dead. I felt like a jellyfish collapsed in a messy heap on the beach. Without firing a shot, the boy panicked, afraid he really had killed me (he later confessed this), and ran away.

"Well," the boy angel continued, "that was one of us."

"What?" I cried wide-eyed, realizing that the lucky *Awaiku* didn't age. Then I flashed back to the trauma with the gun. "What's wrong with you? You scared me to death." I struck my arm out to give the darker one, Keola, a swat. He laughed and darted away, but not before my hand swished through his forearm as if it wasn't there. This reminded me that of course, in reality, he was ethereal.

"That's why we're not telling you which one of us held that

gun, so you won't know who to blame," he said.

My so-called angels laughed and high-fived each other, hands going right through their friend's hand. The taller one, Kainoa, said, "You're hard to get through to at times, so we had to go to an extreme. But didn't that make you dump the bad boyfriend?" I conceded they were right. When my boyfriend blamed me for the stick-up, even I, the greatest doormat that ever lived, sent him the way of all trash.

"Hey, guys," I said, shaking my head at their high spirits, "I admit you are right. And I do thank you for toning it down with the death threats for the last few years. I promise to listen to all the lessons you have for me, so you don't need to use high drama. I like what we did today on our walk—the parking lot construction, the light under the bridge, the crane and the ocean. See? I'm listening."

They nodded and kept close to me all the way home, their eyes full of the usual mischief.

Dear reading public, be sure and ask for the specific *Awaiku* you want. Come to think of it, the tutus might be best after all. But you might want to take a walk with a teen angel once in awhile to keep track of what they're up to.

Respectfully submitted with aloha,

Cate Burns

Chapter 28
Dragon Fruit and Dark Moon

"Hello, Moon! Do you see me down here, night-blooming Cereus? I'm the big yellow blossom that opens out to you in the deepest part of the darkness in May and June." Cereus patiently waited for the moon to respond, then continued. "In Hawaii. You must remember our little romance on the beach at Waikiki. We met at a conference of The Invisible Ones United. Last year. Of course, only your dark side attended, but that was the part that really got to me, so deep and mysterious. I would say tall, dark and handsome if it weren't such a cliché."

Cereus looked up at the sky; she knew the dark side of the moon could hear her special vibrations. They had worked out the code as they lay in a sandy embrace watching a slow tide advance. At last, she heard a faint incoming signal. Oh, how wonderful. He hadn't forgotten her.

"Ye-e-s," he said slowly, his orbit facing away from her as

165

usual. "I remember your thick succulent leaves, almost like a cactus," he chuckled. "But with a very sweet center."

"It's so nice to hear from you, Dark Moon. I have big news," Cereus quickly exclaimed while she had an audible signal.

"Wha-a-at?" she faintly heard.

"I had babies this year, lots of them. And some look like you. Do you remember that I told you my babies are the Dragon Fruits? Well, some of the tiny Dragons are dark. I kiss them every day for you."

"Wo-o-nderfu-u-l. I must come see my beautiful babies." Suddenly his signal came in clear and strong, as sometimes happens. "But are they accepted among your kind, Cereus? You are such a bright delicious sun color. No wonder I loved you so, my opposite darling. How will my dark babies ever have equality and the same educational opportunities as all the other yellow children?"

"I won't lie to you, my dark heart, it might not be easy. First I have to hide the babies from the human women who come early in the morning to steal them. Our dark beauties are prized for their superior nutrition. But you know we live at Punahou school, Barack Obama's alma mater. I am hiding our little Dragon jewels under the long stickers on my leaves; I will keep them safe. And when they grow bigger, they will get the best education in the world. This is America; any one of them could be president of the United States. Imagine, the first Dragon

Fruit/Dark Moon president! How proud we would be."

"If anyone can raise a Dragon Fruit/Dark Moon president, it is you, my dear. Your stickers, dear Cereus, bring back such fond memories of your prickly edges. That's what attracted me to you. I love a challenge. In the end, you retracted all your thorns, so we could become close. You won my black soul. I don't mind being invisible when I can be close to you."

"Oh, you always were the biggest flirt," Cereus said, blushing a faint pink over her yellow petals. "When will you come to Hawaii again, dear one?"

Reception crackled from a passing asteroid. "So-o-n," he said dimly. "They never miss me at work, since no one ever sees me. It's easy to duck out now and then. I will see you before long, my lo-o-ve. Kiss my ba-a-bies."

Medicine Wheel North
The Life Divine

On the traditional Native American medicine wheel, the North symbolizes spiritual life: ways to become free of ego, how to establish a relationship with nature and other powers greater than oneself, sources of wisdom. We find amusement, enthusiasm, inspiration and great potential freedom in the North. We discover prayer and learn how take ourselves less seriously.

I study Buddhism with two Tibetan lamas, and they are the funniest people I know. Although they don't let me get away with much, they've shown me how to laugh in spite of my seemingly eternal placement on the low end of the learning curve.

Chapter 30
Grieving with Underwear

I'm sure I am not the only person who has turned to underwear for solace while grieving. The morning after my mother died, a frigid January day in Seattle, I desperately dug through Mom's closet to find her wool socks and long-johns. I had hurriedly arrived from Honolulu and shivered uncontrollably. My other siblings rolled their eyes when I mentioned our mother's undergarments; I had carte blanche. Six inches taller than Mom with a completely different body type, I didn't imagine any of her clothes might fit me. Later, although it seemed a little creepy at the time, I felt such a need to be close to her that I donned a bra and was shocked at its perfect fit. I didn't tell anyone else about it, but it felt good to carry her scent close to my heart. With her stockings and thin silk pantaloons under my jeans, I felt cocooned in some fragment of her essence. At night I wore her neck-to-ankle nightgowns, swathed in closeness to her twenty-four hours a day.

To tell the truth, while I loved Mom, ours was a deeply problematic relationship at the best of times. For years, I had worked through the issues with therapists and with her, so I felt blessedly free of guilt in the weeks after her unexpected death from a quick cerebral blood clot. I naturally sobbed and mourned her loss, but I was shocked at my need to cuddle near the cloth that had been closest to her skin. However, I accepted the comfort and warmth they gave me. Besides, I continued to find it incredible that we shared the same bra size: my astounding little secret.

But I had no idea that I would target underclothing in times of loss as a general personality trait until several years later when I sadly had to end a long relationship. My first act was to throw out all of my dainties and night wear. He and I had worn t-shirts to bed; into the trash they all went. I bought all new intimate wear and for the first time in my adult life, I became a nightgown owner (like Mom). How cleansed and refreshed I felt to know he wouldn't recognize the inner me or my nighttime self. In my fragile state of mind, this seemed to be a healthy way to establish a bracing authentic identity, separate from him. It worked (along with numerous other self-help efforts, therapy and a final good-bye).

Ten years later, when I broke up with a boyfriend, I saw this pattern reassert itself. Due to a skin condition, I had stopped wearing anything beneath my clothes (or at night) for several years. The skin problem eventually healed, but I had gotten used to the easy and light feeling of wearing a single layer of clothing. But once this relationship ended, the urge to make big changes on the inmost level overcame me in a rush. Similar to what I felt when my long relationship concluded, I needed to claim my interior self as totally my own, unknown and unrecognizable to the person who had intimately known me and yet betrayed me. Off I went to indulge in elegant lingerie, a radical exploration into an unknown me.

Little did I know, but thus began my Great Underpants Search. After several years, much to my dismay, women's personal wear styles had changed. For weeks, I tried this type or that, but could not find a comfortable one. Eventually, I determined that if I combined the feature of one with a section of another and added several pieces of my own fabric, I would have the perfect outcome: artistic panty collages. I hauled out my sewing machine and began to remodel store-bought drawers. Not only would my ex-boyfriend never suspect what I looked like under my dresses, shirts and pants, no one would, for I designed small clothes never before seen on earth in my own unique colors and designs: black and white polka dots with yellow patches and black lace (*à la* Minnie Mouse), a subtle lavender abstract design with gray silk outlined with tiny piping (for business), blue abstract expressionist swirls on black (to wear at the art museum), green Hawaiian sea turtles swimming around a frothy turquoise background (for every day use in Hawaii). Comfort remained the first priority, but colors and textures ran a close second.

Hours of toil on the sewing machine, while listening to old radio comedy shows, proved better and cheaper than therapy; I averaged two pair per one-hour episode. I went a little overboard, sewing fourteen and still counting. My collaged undies provided a fresh feeling, a first chakra celebration of the independent me. Underneath the usual exterior, I vibrated with new effervescence, one that no ex would ever recognize.

As I considered marketing my creations, many names sprang to mind: Peerless Rear, Ultimate Undies, Diva Drawers, Drama Down Below, Betrayal Blast, Nether-regions Nonpareil, Underwear Extraordinaire, Fun Buns. I must admit to a parcel of revenge inherent in these ultra-personal innovations, for they seemed to shout, "Hey, you guys, here is the wild beauty and excitement you are now missing." I'm not proud of this sentiment; vengeance perpetuates negativity, which weighs down our sad world enough as it is. But on the other hand, a small dose of healthy and creative reaction is better than dropping into hysteria or a frozen and blank mind, other options I have tried and would not recommend.

Maybe my next date will have x-ray vision and immediately

174

see the glorious sensually creative inner me with full appreciation that will never wane. What a lovely fairy tale (tail). In reality, I would be satisfied with a slow discovery and enjoyment of the real me; meanwhile, I thoroughly enjoy my inventive thrills on my own.

Let me tell you about the latest wonder: a sedate business-casual paisley set on a background of florescent pink and lime green with a trim of dotted guinea hen feathers (for writing).

I can't wait to see what will happen when I start on bras.

Chapter 31
Codger's Houseboat from Hell

When we boarded a houseboat for a week of wandering on Lake Powell, no one knew that our captain, a retired airline pilot, had a touch of Alzheimers. By the third day we had named him Captain Ahab. By the fourth day, we mutinied.

I signed up for this adventure with my older cousin's kayaking club, knowing it was their swan song before the club disbanded; the members were in their late sixties and seventies with one in his eighties: a jolly crew, all retired from various jobs from teamster to teacher. My extroverted, rugged-faced cousin loved to talk politics; the kayakers must have been accustomed to him, and possibly some individuals enjoyed him. Introvert that I am, I avoided a sixteen-hour car trip from Seattle with my cousin by flying to Salt Lake City to meet up with him.

Conrad was easy to spot with his truck festooned with

several kayaks. We drove a couple of hours to Havasu and by then I was ready for our arrival, knowing that the size of the group would diffuse my cousin's beloved but constant voice.

Our trip began pleasantly enough. I enjoyed the friendly group while privately wondering how one woman, Janice, so wide in girth, could fit in a kayak. With a profile akin to Java the Hutt, she mostly stayed in one place, observed the scene and ate snacks. She was, it turned out, a quite agreeable person.

We quickly noticed the captain's tendency to ram the beach or dock whenever we landed, and I learned to hang onto the closest piece of boat structure at these times. Janice was well-anchored wherever she sat. This group was of an age that still revered airline pilots, so it took a day or so before anyone began to question our esteemed captain's tactics. By the second day, I peered over his shoulder when we were close to land and noticed his limited choice of gears: full speed in both forward and reverse. Others began to frown, especially when he left a couple of folks on the beach, and they had to run through the water to catch hold of the boat. They were dragged along some distance before they managed to haul themselves onto the moving vessel, muttering and cursing. Although outdoor types, we were no longer robust teenagers.

A bunch of us cornered Stella, a nurse and our gentle group organizer. She had chosen Captain Ahab, not knowing of his ailment. She was the logical one to demote him to second mate or, ideally, to no mate. My cousin, an engineer and owner of an array of canoes, kayaks and one small motor boat was the likely substitute. She prepared her speech and promised to speak to the captain before we took off the next morning. Meanwhile, when he rammed a dock, the unsuspecting elderly Diane, wife to the teamster, wasn't holding onto anything, and she fell flat on the back of her head. Her husband, Stan, turned a bright shade of red, his jaw muscles performing a silent workout while he helped his wife up. She protested, saying she was "...just fine. Don't worry." But all of us participants did.

The next morning, Diane indeed felt good, much to our collective relief. Before we set out, a smiling Stella informed us she had a frank discussion with the captain and he admitted he "wasn't quite up to the task." He had graciously let Stella assign a substitute. We all heaved a great communal sigh of joy. A difficult task completed, we could relax and savor the wondrous red sandstone and sparkling waters of Lake Powell. But when breakfast dishes were washed and put away and our departure time of nine a.m. arrived, so did Captain Ahab, who placed his hands on the captain's wheel and started the engine while we—especially Stella—stared openmouthed. She gingerly approached the captain, while the rest of us stood behind her.

"Captain? We have Conrad here to drive the boat today, like we talked about before breakfast." She gestured toward my silver-haired rotund cousin. "Here he is."

"Why would he do that?" the Captain asked as he sped away from the dock and I grabbed the nearest wall. "I'm the captain."

"But, don't you remember our talk?" Stella asked, the wild ride forcing her to grab at a cupboard to save herself a fall.

"What talk?" Captain Ahab replied.

We were stuck on a never-ending loop with an eternal Captain Ahab who lacked short-term memory. We took turns hovering over our good captain. He didn't seem to mind when we shoved the gear lower or put our hands on the wheel and turned it toward a safer direction. But it proved socially awkward.

"What are you doing here?" the captain would ask me as I lowered the gear. He had a genuinely curious tone of voice, as if he simply wondered why I stood next to him.

"Oh, just enjoying the view," I said as I turned the wheel to avoid hitting another boat.

This situation wasn't ideal, but, by communal consensus, we banded together and helped Captain Ahab. Stan abstained from helping, continuing to mutter, complain and stay at a distance, as if trying to keep himself from tying up our captain. And I didn't blame him; his wife had taken a hit. But even he didn't seem to think it was worth forfeiting his money and abandoning the trip.

The beach landings were interesting: high, low, high, low

gears, as the boat lurched ashore with the captain and his shadow non-captain not working together. We muddled through, that is until Susan, a retired parks commissioner, broke her leg in multiple places. Miraculously, Captain Ahab didn't do it.

Unfortunately, we were at the far end of the lake, one-half day away from the nearest civilization. We had unloaded our kayaks on a wide beach; I was next to Susan when I saw her slip on the slanted sandy bank. Down she went. I wouldn't have worried, except that her descent was accompanied by the sickening crunches of bones breaking. I rushed to her and called out to others nearby. We carried her to the boat and set up a bed where she could elevate her leg. Stella, as the nurse on board, took over while I fetched ice and held it on Susan's injury.

Captain Ahab had fewer guardians now.

A retired architect, Brian, a blond man of Irish heritage, frequently seen with a bottle in his hand, spent more time with the captain, as did my cousin, Conrad. Stella's husband, Mack, in his eighties, tried to help the captain, but he was too nice to take the wheel and jerk it out of the captain's hands. We were not a jolly crew. Out of cell-phone range, we examined maps and headed toward the nearest dock with a taxi that could get Susan to a doctor.

Hours later, Captain Ahab, with several other people

hanging on the wheel, managed to dock the boat without hitting anything. Brian hailed a taxi. Hazy with painkillers and unrelenting pain, Susan allowed herself to be carried ashore and laid in a taxi. Brian accompanied Susan to a doctor, while cell phones buzzed to put Susan's family on alert. The rest of us on board relaxed and had a beer or lemonade; the worst was over, we thought.

However, we had to go to another dock for the night to refuel and Captain Ahab automatically took over while the rest of us apparently forgot our captain-oversight duties. By the time we got to the long dock, it was dark and the slips were almost all full. I was down in my tiny sleeping compartment at the water line when I felt a shudder and crash, and realized I should be on deck with the captain. When this was followed by another crunch and loud screams, and yet another bang, I ran upstairs. Stella and Conrad were wresting the steering wheel and gear shift out of our captain's hands. The yells hailed from the neighboring boat we repeatedly hit. I threw up my arms as if to shield myself from the new drama. This time, Captain Ahab had done real damage. Other boat owners appeared and sided with the damaged boat's owner, rightly so. A mob assembled. Conrad, my politically experienced cousin, and Stella, with her caring logic, were on active duty. I hoped Conrad's extensive powers of monologue might quell the general hysteria.

Munching on a new snack, Janice stayed in the spot she had occupied all day. I wished I could share her impressive implacability (without the calories).

I saw Brian sidle on board. He had delivered Susan into the doctor's care, found us and returned to this dismal scene. When he saw the mess, which now involved the police, he scampered away. I stayed to watch in mute horror as the wronged boat owner howled her unbelief and dismay while her friends and neighbors added their eyewitness accounts and hearty emotions. Conrad and Stella persevered against the odds, their calm tones sounded like the quiet slide of ocean water up the beach after a wave's roar.

I guess we had gotten used to our captain's handicap, but, naturally, the other boat owners had no such compassion and understanding for what looked like multiple intentional crashes into their boat. Captain Ahab gazed at the scene with a dispassionate eye and no apparent comprehension. At last, Stella, Conrad and the police sorted things out and commenced paperwork, which would take hours.

Mack looked on and I joined him. "What do you think, Mack?"

He gave his sweet smile, "It's a mess, that's for sure. But Stella will iron it out. She always does." I believed him.

I walked back toward the stairs, thinking of my tiny bed where I could put my head under a pillow; between Susan's horror and a boat wreck, my reclusive personality craved oblivion. On the way down, I saw Stan and Diane. He blustered, "This is it. I've had it. We are leaving this disaster. This man is too dangerous." Numerous expletives accompanied his outburst.

With tremendous powers of persistence, Diane unsuccessfully tried to placate him. "We can't leave the group. It's going to be okay, honey, you'll see." But he ignored her.

Mutiny.

When I turned the corner to the last set of stairs into the hold of the boat where my little bed lay, to my surprise, Brian, far from his room, crouched on the floor at the bottom of the stairs, cradling a bottle. "Brian, are you hiding from us?" I asked with incredulous curiosity.

He took a swig and mumbled something about "...police... search boat."

"Are you fourteen years old, trying to keep your liquor away from your mother?" I asked. Then I thought a moment, "Are you wanted? Or have drugs?" The stress of the day and the absurdity of Brian huddled on the floor overcame me as I sank down to a step and burst out laughing. A small smile quirked the edges of his mouth up, as if he was a teenager caught by his mom who had decided not to punish him.

I laughed until my ribs ached, hunkered down next to a drunk who had just taken his friend to the emergency room, trapped on a boat with a truly insane captain who we had all tried to accommodate, the ultimate enablers. I heard the voices of the police questioning, the wronged boat owner still yelling in righteous indignation every so often (understandably), my cousin negotiating, and Stella's compassionate explanations. As I watched Brian drinking, I imagined Mack praying.

All at once, I saw us as a boat-load of oldsters stuck together, each of us coping with nature run amuck. When you think of it, this could be a definition of what happens in old age. A great god of gerontology mixed us up in a petri dish and put us *in extremis* to see how many responses he could elicit in aged *homo sapiens*.

Stan chose anger; it spewed out at the first adversity.

His wife, Diane, placated and lived in her illusion that "Everything is okay. Just don't make a fuss." A perfect pair.

Stella, the caretaker, helped the group with her social skills, medical knowledge and her clear thinking.

Her husband, Mack, shone with a sweet spiritual faith.

Janice ate.

Susan personified physical helplessness.

Captain Ahab went crazy.

Brian drank reality away.

My cousin organized, mediated and used filibuster when necessary.

I flitted here and there, a gadfly, until my need to escape

185

took over.

We each personified archetypes of disparate temperament types with the god of gerontology, no doubt, taking notes. "Humans faced chaos in the following ten categories, listed below," he probably wrote on his Excel spread sheet, including a personality profile of each individual.

Tapping the keys, he might have pondered, "These traits will probably predict how they will handle the ultimate ignoble dictum I have cast upon them: death."

After a moment of thought, he might give a satisfied grin. "This houseboat has been good practice for them. Look at the creative array of their solutions. They can learn from each other." The god of gerontology was an optimist.

The next morning, half our group stalked off, waddled away or flew, air-lifted on a stretcher.

The co-dependents, the drunk, the nutcase and the penny-pinchers stayed together, as natural a crew as could be found: Stella and Mack, my cousin and I, and Brian. And, of course, Captain Ahab who later happily paid for the damages he caused. After several surgeries, Susan walked again. Our captain drifted into amiable insanity. We, more or less, survived the god's experiment on the codgers' houseboat from hell.

Chapter 32
Punxsutawney Phil

Punxsutawney Phil, a handsome groundhog with a long aristocratic nose, scuttled backward into his hole when he felt the ground tremble with Black Wolf's approach.

"Wait a minute, Phil," howled the sleek Black Wolf who had been tracking the large rodent for weeks. Black Wolf's fur coat shone in the moonlight, illuminating the stars and moon back to themselves.

Phil backed farther down into his hole, leaving one eye on Black Wolf, or "BW" as he called him. "My intuition says not to trust you any farther than I can spit, and that's two feet."

In a philosophical mood, having just eaten a rabbit, BW said, "You, my dear friend Phil, must aspire to and commit to the great virtue of releasing your fears so that you might ascend to the next spiritual level."

"Well, BW, I do better than you. Humans turn to me to help

them tell time. With all my especially honed clout over the seasons, I inform humans when spring has truly arrived."

"I admit you have amazing powers of focus on time and the seasons. But as a visionary, I can imagine a seashell balanced on top of a mountain lake. Therefore, I can decide what is, in fact and in metaphor, true," said BW with a haughty toss of his head.

"Well, you can't dig holes with great earthmoving force like I can," Phil said as he dug his toenails into the soil. "You see, I bring harmony to the underworld, aerating the soil for all the millions of bugs and microbes who transform dirt into the magic needed to grow plants that feed your prey that feeds you, Mister Smarty."

BW looked at the skinny moon hanging in the sky like a smile. He lifted his nose and howled a lonely sound. "We have double harmony together. I work with the moon and her seasons of tide and light."

"Okay, okay, we both have our strengths," said Phil, who, throughout this conversation had slowly relaxed and inched out of his hole to talk to BW. Nothing escaped BW's sharp predator nose and eyes. Before Phil could register what had happened, BW had pounced on him and held his neck between his jaws.

"Help," Phil screeched through a closing throat. "Stop that!" Phil lashed out a sharp digging claw and raked BW's eye and cheek, opening a large gash.

BW, partially blinded, jumped back, "Hey, I was only kidding."

"Tell that to Darwin, you hunter, you," Phil said, scurrying back into his hole.

"Yeah, yeah, I know, nature and nurture and all that. But I'm not only a predator. I can dream of world peace, and I can even help you, little Phil."

"How can you help me?" Phil asked stretching out the crick in his neck where BW had held it in his grasp.

BW looked up at the moon again. "I can decide to be determined and to be wise, to make it my destiny to explore the unknown, the part of me who is not a predator."

Phil rubbed his sore neck. "In your dreams," he said. "You meat-eaters are all alike. You will never have the refined sensibilities and impeccability of us herbivores. We understand the grief at the essence of all those who are prey—us. We know this in the deep silence of our being. We grieve every day for our loved ones you have eaten."

"But I am innocent, too," cried BW. "I have no choice about hunting and eating. I have to go with the flow and mystery of the great force that made me eat meat and made me cull out the weak and old animals that are the easiest to catch, helping your friend Darwin along."

"Well, you don't have to do that all the time. My grandmother was old and weak, but I still didn't want you to eat her. So, give us a break some of the time. Hone your skills and use your creativity; try a veggie meal today, and then again tomorrow. Use your ingenuity to look around you and gather up protein-rich plants. I'll give you some recipes so you can share them with your family."

"Look, when I eat another animal, before the first chomp, I center myself and pray for the animal, making it an offering to the Great Spirit that made me a meat-eater. But I understand it's all a matter of balance. In the interest of our enduring friendship, I'll eat a veggie meal each day, too."

Phil gulped. "We have a friendship? What does that mean exactly? That you won't eat me?"

"Not until you are so old or sick that you give me permission to help you out with my especially quick neck snap, to assist you into the other world easily."

Phil rubbed his neck. "And before your quick neck snap, will you center yourself and pray for me and tell me a joke the second before you do it? I want to die laughing."

"Sure," BW said. "I know some good groundhog jokes."

"Nothing demeaning," said Phil. "I have my pride." Phil thought for a moment longer. "And you're sure you won't eat me willy-nilly someday because you forgot your promise?"

"I'll do even better than that. I promise to eat no groundhogs at all until one of them asks me to help him out with the neck trick. Now, Phil, about those groundhog jokes, have you heard the one about how many groundhogs it takes to screw in a light bulb?"

"You've got to do better than that, Black Wolf. Tell me another one," Phil said as he relaxed his long furry body and lay down in the entrance, eager to hear a new joke.

Chapter 33
Party Tricks

Mom lived for parties and would do anything to liven one up. When she found out a distant cousin, Roland, an unusual chiropractor, used hypnotism with his patients, nothing would do but for him to hypnotize her friends at the next party. She'd be the talk of the neighborhood.

After Roland got Don Sorenson to gobble like a turkey whenever anyone said his name, Mom was on a real hypnotism kick. She claimed it was the modern way of the future, and maybe it was—in the 1950s. Somehow, she found a dentist, Dr. Gottlieb, to hypnotize my sisters and me for all our dental work. To this day, I have an unnatural love of dentists.

Then Mom got the idea that she would look like an avant-garde parent (artists were worshipped at our house) if Roland taught her kids self-hypnosis. I would have preferred dinner to hypnosis. But Mom always looked for ways to brag about us, and at ten years old, I liked it when she did.

Roland was a small quiet man, soft and white as a melting vanilla ice cream cone and just as sweet. He rarely spoke and when he did, his voice was low. I had to bend near to catch his words. He had a pudgy stomach and I could count the few individual wispy hairs that stuck straight up atop his shiny head. I felt safe with Roland. He laughed at Mom's continual stream of jokes, just like I did; we were united in our desire to please her.

Roland spent a whole afternoon with me alone, explaining hypnotism. Overwhelmed by the headlight glare of an adult's single focus on me, I sat straight and leaned all my efforts toward him. An adult had never sat with me one on one for so long before. He didn't talk down to me; he seemed to expect me to understand, and I thought I did.

He taught me that the key to the whole endeavor was to learn how to relax, an alien concept in our hyper household. He showed me how to calm myself by feeling each breath and counting it, one by one. Dr. Gottlieb, the dentist, did the same thing. Numbering my breaths helped me to become quiet in my brain. In this state, I could look at my thoughts and notice that some were good and some weren't. Roland said I shouldn't mentally repeat the bad ones, like how ashamed I was each time I wet the bed, because it could make me wet the bed more often.

In hypnosis, the good experiences, like the rare joy of waking up in a dry bed, were to be as savored as a big Christmas present. Once I relaxed, I could repeat the best mental pictures and feelings in my mind, and they would really come true someday. Roland said I could dream up good thoughts, even write them ahead of time so they were ready once I was deep at rest. I quickly made lists in my puffy vinyl pink "Daily Diary" of all I wanted.

Roland didn't sigh and look around to see where Mom was the way most adults did with me. While he listed all the techniques to use, he didn't explain why a child should hypnotize herself. And I never thought to ask. Who would question Mom's will? You would think a kid would be eager to know how to make her friends gobble on command, but Roland didn't teach me and it didn't occur to me to wonder. I was wholly captivated by his special secrets of the mind, which made me feel as if I were being inducted into an exclusive initiation ceremony like a bat mitzvah or a *quinciniera*, neither of which I would ever experience. Roland, in a single hypnosis lesson, ended up providing my only rite of passage out of childhood.

Perhaps I had a premonition of this, or maybe I simply coveted being the center of someone's—anyone's—attention, but the result was that I fell in love with hypnosis. Every day in my quiet times, I rested, counted my breaths and focused on the good thoughts I had prepared, repeating them in my mind as many times as I could. I got really good stuff that way. I stopped wetting the bed. My ankle hardly hurt when I broke it. I got rid of all my warts. I loved going to the dentist.

Once Roland finished my lesson, I don't remember Mom ever referring to my hypnosis abilities again. Perhaps I disappointed her fantasies of having an in-house party trickster hypnotist. I was never adept at extroversion, much to Mom's eternal disappointment. Instinctively, I kept my love of hypnotism a secret from her.

Years later, when I got to the university and studied Buddhism, I found I had been meditating like the Zen Buddhists: relaxing and slowing thoughts, observing my mind, counting breaths, choosing the positive. Glory be. This was my own personal miracle. I kept reading about Buddhism and meditation and I learned that when I stood back from my thoughts and observed them, I could let them dissolve and be free of them. The kind of stuff my mind drones on and on about is exactly what you'd want to make disappear. "I want a chocolate bar. Now. Will the cute guy in the front row look at me? I want a chocolate bar. Now." *Ad nauseum*. Like an obsessive fisherman casting the line all day without a bite, the ego tape loops seemed to be a satisfying end unto themselves. But once in awhile, my mind was rewarded by a bite of chocolate or a glance from a boy. Oddly enough, with meditation, I wanted fewer chocolate bars each day. Lust, I am glad to report, did not diminish. Apparently, I was not nun material.

I continued to hold my hypnotism/meditation interests close to my heart and out of Mom's way, for she was an atheist and proud of it. Hypnosis might have been okay in her book, but meditation equaled Buddhism. She ridiculed all religions: Christians believed in a bunch of fairy tales, Hindus worshipped statues, Buddhists were selfish, only out for their own enlightenment. I wanted her love too much to have conflict over something so important to me and I knew enough to avoid becoming Mom's target. I wouldn't dare join a temple. Even when I got a degree in Asian Studies, I told her I studied Far Eastern politics; the Vietnam war provided me with credibility.

Some years later, I took courses in Hypnosis and Self-Hypnosis and learned that I had to hand it to Roland; he had taken the time to teach a little kid the correct basics. Over the years, I had gotten used to the benefits and was selfish enough to continue to use self-hypnosis as a mental bedrock, a way to check in each day and feel solid and centered within. Along the way, it aided my concentration in school, reduced some illnesses and fears, and helped me unwind at night. I have infinite gratitude to Roland for giving a small child a precious gift that seemed magically to produce such lovely fruits. And, of course, I must thank Mom for her cockamamie enthusiasms that made her wrangle hypnosis lessons from Roland.

In the late 1990s, I lived in Honolulu and continued my self-hypnosis and meditation practice. I read every book I could find on hypnosis and Buddhism, but still kept my Buddhist beliefs underground. Even though we lived in different states, Mom's opinions on religion were sharp as ever. I mostly avoided the scimitar of her fundamentalist atheism until she passed into wherever it is that atheists go after death. I refused to linger on this line of inquiry as I figured her atheist's afterlife might be nowhere.

Much to my surprise, I showed up on the doorstep of a Buddhist temple shortly after Mom's death. For the first time, I enjoyed the thrill of being able to meditate in public. Within weeks, I became an out-of-the-closet Buddhist, a card-carrying member of a temple in Honolulu. I joined their choir and poured my heart into Buddhist songs with a loud voice after so many years of silence. We sang a full range of global music: Eastern and Western styles of classical and folk music, and also contemporary jazz and gospel-style works, in both Japanese and English. I loved it all.

Today, when I belt out Buddhist music, I smile, knowing I have come full circle, celebrating hypnotism/meditation with my kind of party; different from Mom's bashes, but linked in spirit. I now realize that, with me, Roland pulled off the greatest party trick of all.

Chapter 34
Alarm

I give regular tours at a contemporary art museum. One day when I enter the museum, I hear the dreadful sound of a car alarm coming from a back gallery. It sounds as if the classic screeching sound track alternates every 60 seconds or so, from European ambulance siren sounds (no doubt taken from World War II movies that featured Nazis hunting Anne Frank), to the deafening beeps of a truck backing up, to a loud computerized electronic stutter. My innards clench as my mind begins a litany of negativity: "I hate that damn noise. How could those people (car owners/alarm companies) be so cruel as to torture the public like this? These horrible things must be in violation of city decibel ordinances. Their creators belong in jail."

Thus I enter the back gallery with my mouth puckered in disapproval, my jaw grinding in a way that will cause repercussions with my TMJ dentist. That's when I see the video that accompanies the cacophony.

On the video screen, a modern dancer has choreographed her own personal disco moves using the car alarm as a score. With joyful abandon, she does a 1960s rock and roll classic, pumping her arms up and down like pistons and swaying her hips to the Nazi ambulance sounds. With the piercing truck-back-up blasts, she kicks her legs up and adds a swimmer's back-stroke with her arms. To the computerized electronic stutters, she dances a robot-style Charleston. A big smile replaces my Calvinist judgments.

My urban apartment faces a large parking lot. Inevitably, those old car alarms still occasionally detonate. But now, every time, I laugh, remembering the exuberant dance. And, if no one is watching, my arms and legs twitch with a little robotic Charleston of my own.

Chapter 35
Conversations with Kuan Yin

I sat in front of my home altar with a white porcelain statue of a graceful and beautiful Asian woman in front of me. "My dear Buddhist sage," I murmured, "I know you are always with me. When I pause for a moment, I hear messages from you imprinted on my inner ear, ones that no one else can hear. You must remember that I bought a full-length scroll of you when I was eighteen years old. Before I knew your name, I carried you with me everywhere I moved. That's why I have thought that I was always tuned in to you, listening and learning.

"But, looking back on my life, I have to wonder about certain events. For example, why did you allow me to stay with a bully for years? Couldn't you have let me date him for just a little while? You, of all people, could have discerned more subtle ways to persuade me to take you seriously."

I heard a voice caressing my consciousness. "No, you are

too pigheaded and lazy. I needed him to cut through your illusion of being Ms. Nice Girl all the time, to get you serious about taking good care of yourself. And to remind you to listen to me instead of the sweet-talking guy. You are lucky I didn't send you a psychopath."

"You may have a good point there, dear Buddha head. Spending years with him was perhaps a bit excessive. But it seems to me that life is a balance of listening to your great advice and then plunging ahead with my own instincts. He was the sweetest, most generous, thoughtful and kind man I had ever met—at first." I sigh, remembering my handsome lover during our courtship.

"And didn't that change immediately after you moved in and opened a joint bank account?" my Bodhisattva conscience ruthlessly persisted.

"Well, yes, you are right. But the poor thing began to suffer from suicidal tendencies," I said. "I know I was a sap to believe him and cater to his every wish to protect him from stress. The last year we were together, he admitted he had made it all up. And I'd thought I was such a good person to help him with all his troubles."

"You were, my dear idiot. But what might the lesson be?" Kuan Yin persevered.

"Oh, I get so tired of lessons, lessons, lessons," I moaned.

"You aren't used to it yet, dear? This is as good as it gets.

And you're lucky to be getting the lessons. May I remind you of the alternative?" My Buddhist saint's patience seemed to be wearing thin.

"But do you have to make the lessons so difficult?" I whined. "Why the hard-drinking mother? Really. That was too much for a child to bear. And all those horrible illnesses. Yuck."

"Lessons, dear girl, what were they?" My tender lady of ultimate compassion did not stop the interrogation, no matter how maudlin I became.

"I get it. Learn to take good care of myself first, not the drunk mom, not the fake-suicidal guy. My last round of illness, I coddled myself just the way you wanted me to, didn't I?" I asked her.

"You just might be save-able after all. And what other lesson, little one? You are missing a major point, here." If my porcelain statue could have impatiently tapped her foot on the ground, she would have.

"Oh, man," I scratched my head and furrowed my thick eyebrows together. All at once, I looked up, as if my invisible guardian Buddhist angel floated above me. "Oh, my god, I did it again, didn't I? I set an authority figure high up on a pedestal for me to worship. You. I did the same thing with Mom and with several ex-boyfriends. As I bemoaned my terrible karma, I gave you all the power, as if you were responsible for me. I know darn well none of you make my fate. I do."

Little Ms. Muffet sat on a tuffet, eating her curds and whey.

Along came a....

"I know, I know. I invite them in; the spider and the big bad wolf. I kowtow, giving them an invitation to victimize me at will." I pounded my fist on my thigh. "Never again. I've had it. No more giving away my power. No more predators allowed."

My exquisitely robed Asian companion of the mind laughed and clapped her hands, nearly knocking her halo askew. "Well, my dear, you just did it again with me. But at least you saw it and stopped; that's the main thing. Next time you'll see it and stop again." She put up her palm for a high five and I gave her one, but I accidently pushed her so hard she fell off her koa wood altar and bounced several feet along the carpet. A finger and toe snapped off. I left her there. We each learn humility in our own way.

Chapter 36
Purple Prejudice

My hidden secret is that the color purple pops out in importance throughout my life. I can't keep it down. As an artist, I officially don't believe in having a favorite color. All artists and relativists such as Heisenberg know that hue (and a human down to the atomic level) changes depending on context. The color blue looks different when placed next to orange. And the same can be said of any color in interaction with its surroundings. But my life experience proclaims, "Purple trumps."

Years ago when I was in a hospital isolation ward with adult mumps, both cheeks swollen like a chipmunk transporting a bounty of nuts, I was bereft of human company for ten days except for a quarantine nurse, fully swathed in white from the top of her head down to her thick spongy shoes. This ghostly apparition pushed a tray of food and juice at me from a distance three times a day. Gloriously, the juice was from Concord grapes. After seven days, practically snow-blind in this environment, I allowed the divine dense color of the nectar to take over my will. The nurses never said a word when, for the last several days of my incarceration, I spilled long splatters of purple all around me and was enfolded in a scented abstract painting. I spent happy mindless hours gazing and inhaling.

Two decades later, the day arrived when I tired of my spotted and stained white blouses and underwear. Not wanting to donate them to the thrift store (my depression era parents' voices still shrill in my mind), I found bottles of purple dye at the drug store and filled my washing machine with this majestic hue. In went all my whites. What swirling, sumptuous purples came into being: blouses, skirts, bras, underpants that make me laugh whenever I wear them. Purple is not an unusual color these days, but every time I wear one of my hand-dyed shirts, I get compliments.

Purple is a secondary color, made by mixing two primary colors: red and blue. All secondary colors have an otherworldly quality. When we eventually meet space aliens, they are likely to be green, orange, purple or a combination of these. From my ethereal life down to the physical, my very cells are defined by the purples: the rich antioxidants of the wild blueberries and blackberries I feasted on in my childhood backyard. More recently, acai berries, black rice, Molokai potatoes and eggplant regularly digested into sinew.

In foods too long on the vine or in the fridge, purple is also the color of rotted areas on vegetables or moldy spots on bread, a vital part of joyous fermentation (think wine, dark beers and sauerkraut) and otherwise recycled life. Deadly nightshade grows in abundance in my childhood home in Seattle, its dark lavender blossoms and bright yellow center alluring to a curious child. I learned early that beauty might hide death; the clever kids, and the ones who wanted to live, avoided dangerous lurking purples.

My Buddhist temple favors lavender and purple colors, from pale wisteria, the symbol of my particular tradition, to the deep purple of royalty connoting Siddhartha as a holy prince. My Buddhist choir sings in purple robes. When I am wrapped in this color from chin to toe, I sing with full gusto, my voice blasting in Buddha's ear.

In meditation, I enter a purple and lavender world behind my eyes, with splatters of pink and navy blue at times. These northern lights of the mind cover me like a warm blanket. The colorful array roams around my third eye where it cancels all thought and allows me to bask in pure peace, just like the meditation masters promise.

My eighth chakra is a lavender-pink with silver. I know this because one odd day, I slipped into it and dwelt there during a conversation I was attempting to have with a German woman in Hamburg. I spoke no German and no drugs altered my mind, not even Konig Pilsener, an epic Teutonic beer. With my total concentration focused on her, I was astounded to find myself continuing the conversation from above my body, encapsulated in a colored sphere, where, once I got over the shock, I felt cozy. Somewhere later in the conversation with the Hamburgian, I slipped back into my corporeal flesh. I don't think she noticed anything amiss, except perhaps an American's stupidity in foreign languages. As much as I would like to revisit my personal happy purple cloud of foreign language expertise, fate has never opened that door to me again.

As a child, I was an inveterate tomboy with a blossoming bruise somewhere on my body at all times, a badge of intense play. But, in late adulthood, I developed a rare autoimmune disease that caused giant four to five inch bruises all over my body, each a miniature Mt. Vesuvius that imparted sensations of skin being seared; as in frying chicken if I were the chicken. I had more than one hundred of these for months with no known cure in Western medicine. I avoided the local Domestic Abuse non-profit's fundraiser that year, which I usually attended. My explanation: "Oh, these bruises just popped up all on their own," would have rung hollow.

Weirdly, my autoimmune bruises looked nothing like my childhood shiners; the new and improved versions made unique circular designs that ebbed and flowed and overlapped. Some resembled concentric, irregularly spaced tree rings, their size depending on that year's rainfall total or, in my case, the ferocity of the attack that day. I gained new respect for what trees go through in their silent way.

With purple my dominant hue, I also featured some red, blue, and black. I could not help but photograph the incredible shapes, and I spent zoned-out hours forging them into collages. It was weird but therapeutic.

Eventually, after almost a year, I found slow alternative medical remedies. Over the months, the bruises subsided, from one hundred to seventy-five, then to fifty, twenty-five, fifteen eight, four, then from four to two. I delineate this boring and slow progression because it defined my life, offering a ponderous endurance contest that seemed to last forever. Which would I lose first, my purple cast or my sanity?

The number range stayed consistent at each level. Having lived on a mountain at 8,000 feet for many years, I had experienced nature's abrupt plateaus of change; it snows two feet less per storm at 7,500 feet as compared to 8,000 feet, where the lucky inhabitants sport larger biceps from shoveling a lot more snow. In my neighborhood, Mother Nature drew a big line in the snow: the higher the level, two feet more. Thus according to the natural world's increments did my small-blood-vessel-self-destruct disease recede back from whence it came, stage by stage. Eventually the blessed day arrived with zero bruises and although the next day might find me with two more, I sobbed for the miracle of new health. The dark hues slowly slid off my body to no doubt, descend back to their hellish origins.

My purple visitations left me contemplating their variety of meanings: pain, survival, learning, growth, beauty, peace. No other color seduces me into such a pantheon, whether the seduction is in pain or in ecstasy.

Chapter 37
Ditto, Zona and Moneycakes

I have an ego named Ditto because she has a loud voice that insists on telling me to do the same things over and over daily: "Work harder. Do it better. Make it bigger. Keep a sparkling house that looks good to visitors. Dress up and go out with friends and impress the crowd. Put your name out there. Network. Get those promotions."

Tall and slender (naturally), with fashionable short, spiky hair, Ditto is quite an optimist. Usually, she embarrasses me when she pushes me into swanky social situations because I've never been one for the quick repost. Ditto knows this, but she is a blind opportunist; reality doesn't stop her. Every situation is one to overcome, go beyond, or machete out of the way.

I am sorry to admit it, since Ditto is after all a major part of me, but she is a money-grubber. In a portrait, her large nose would be a dollar sign. Ditto means well. The picture of her lovely green face features hearts on her cheeks and a big smile; she wants me to have financial security into old age and I admire her goal, if not her means of achieving it.

It all began innocently enough. When I was five years old, the biggest thrill on the block was to have your Mom throw you a big birthday party complete with a money-cake. Oh, how I endlessly begged for a money-cake, the stuff of dreams. This was, of course, the innocent 1950s. Nowadays a cake full of coins would be seen as a vehicle for toxic warfare that could wipe out a neighborhood. But in that more naïve time, on my fifth birthday, my wish came true. I still savor the photographs of the outdoor party in August under the large maple tree, all the neighborhood kids wearing pointed party hats.

In that bygone era, quarters, dimes, nickels and even pennies meant big financial thrills to a child: pop, candy bars, comic books, movies. With delirious anticipation, I studied the whole money-cake creation process from start to finish. Mom poured raw cake batter into two round, flat pans and before baking, sprinkled handfuls of (hopefully washed, but knowing Mom, I doubt it) coins into the gooey mass where they baked into random positions, suspended in the two-layer frosted cake. I don't remember what flavor the cake was. All that mattered was the money.

Although I had not named Ditto at age five, she focused ferocious attention on the intense joy and social elevation the

214

money-cake brought as kids' teeth clanked down on metal amid screams of delight. Ditto learned money was a supreme good. When the children revealed who ended up with the quarters, I learned envy and greed in a big way: the more coins, the better.

I love Ditto dearly, for she has helped me over the years, but, unfortunately, she has never learned when enough is enough. Like a monk repeating mantras, Ditto repeats her litany endlessly. "Work harder. Do it better." She seems to think her way is the ultimate good, the answer to the meaning of life. And I believed her for more years than I care to admit to.

As the decades flew by, a few catastrophes made me sit back on my haunches and wonder if there was more to life than Ditto. I notice that when disaster strikes, Ditto revs up her demands to a hysterical level, "If only you had worked harder." "You should have done it better." When my boyfriend suddenly and unexpectedly died when I was 29 years old, Ditto came unglued, blasting her dogma like a broken video loop on high volume. For the first time, I turned around and looked Ditto in the eye, for I knew I did not have the power over death that she thought she/I had. The problem was, I had believed her for so long, I didn't know how to turn down her volume. So, off I went to a therapist for a year.

Ditto is a hard case, but I have learned that with an ego, the old cliché is actually true: flattery works. Each day, there come times when, for my sanity and peace, I must politely tell Ditto to take a hike. Ditto, as you can imagine is easily offended, so, in reality, several times a day I carefully and sincerely (Ditto instantly knows when I lie) say to her, "You are such a great problem-solver, Ditto. Thank you for all your help today. But now it's time to for me to rest from all your ingenious projects. I'll see you later." Lucky for me, she falls for this truthful line every time. And when she does, I gratefully give myself over to Zona.

Opposite to Ditto, Zona never repeats herself. She is a fount of creativity, my source when I meditate, walk, make art, write or play. Zona is an old woman with shoulder-length silver hair who has kept a wiry strength in her ropy arms and legs. With Zona I completely relax, doze, ruminate and feel my essential energies that gently pulse through every centimeter of my body, like sweet shimmers; the essence of joy.

Whereas Ditto knows how to get errands done and how to balance a checkbook (thank you very much, Ditto; you are the best), Zona shows me bliss. Every part of me is included in her divine rapture, even my lowly foot. If I drew a picture of a Zona foot, it would sparkle with rainbow colors and whirls of foot chakra energy.

With Zona, I thrill at every toe, grateful for the precious appendages. I once knew a very distinguished man at the top of his profession; but someone whispered to me that he had no toes, amputated from diabetes. While trying not to watch him walk, I observed him cross a wide courthouse porch with short, choppy steps, a man of great wealth and local fame, bereft of toes.

I paint and draw these magnificent toe-energies, one by one. I document the happy internal forms of movement; even the humble toe leaves an impression on the world with each move it makes. I tie a string dipped in black or white paint around the joint and ask the forbearing model to move her toe in every possible direction, resulting in an image of what the movement looks like. I had always wondered. As it turns out, the big toe can move a little side to side, as well as up and down, resulting in two elegant diagonal lines swirling in opposite directions.

With great gratitude to Zona for showing me the precious body energies, the sacred source of life, I say:

Zona allows me to buzz, thrill, drone, pulse, each moment magnified,

As if I sit on a tractor that sends vibrations sweeping through skin, muscles and bones.

Zona, the farmer, cultivates every cell.

Does Zona think money-cakes are worthwhile? In 1953, she adored the creativity and fun. She loves to laugh. But Zona knows where to set limits. The other day, she sat me down for a serious talk about money-cakes.

"You have enough already, Cate. Every dream you invested in those money-cakes has come true. You've done it! Now it's time to stop striving for more."

Whoa! She asks me to give up a lifetime of the endless goals that define my life/ambition (one and the same). I had learned to regulate Ditto to give me some rest each day, but to let go of her entire agenda?

"That's asking too much, Zona. Way too much. I love my goals. And it's fashionable for women to haul in the dough these days."

"I hate to break it to you, dear, but money alone isn't the real you. What else is you?" Zona's pale blue-gray eyes narrowed.

It took me several years and a serious illness to finally admit Zona was right. Next, I had to answer her question, "What could be more important to me than my ambitions?" An explorer in a new terrain, I set out to make a map. I had to start with what I knew: Ditto's admonitions. Without telling Ditto, I examined her list, determined to do the opposite and discover the real me. Hence, my new credo:

• Work less. I quit my job and mostly retired.

• Slough off and enjoy it.

• Let the house relax, too. Make a mess.

• Hang out with people I love, not the ones that benefit my career.

• Rest on my laurels, even if they are tiny laurels.

Zona is right. The new me feels terrific. Ditto's still in my life, helping me learn how to spend and not save. She adjusts to the new me with vigor while keeping her eye on those money-cakes so they don't run out before my expiration date. Dependable Ditto.

Chapter 38
Archetype Attacks

<u>The Scene: Pastoral Mountain Idyll</u>

I knew my "sort of" boyfriend, Evan, had ulterior motives when he took me on a surprise visit to a mountain park. We had broken up for a month and, clearly, his plan at this remote park was to find a secluded spot to seduce me back into the relationship. To tell the truth, I liked the idea.

But, like the good girl I have always been, I had set a bedrock boundary with him. No more sex until he banned all secrecy about me with his ex-girlfriend (that he supposedly was not romantically involved with). Why did he need to keep our relationship hidden from his ex? Good question that he claimed not to understand. He just needed a few months to slowly ease away from their emotional bond, for she had needed his help to get a job and a car. I gave him a few months. And he gave me the best sex on the planet. A fair exchange while it lasted.

But four-plus months into it, my accursed self-worth demanded that I take an open and honest place in his world. No more hiding and playing the mistress role. Unfortunately, giving up regular physical bliss, more intense than I had ever experienced before, made me doubt my sanity. Ethics or ecstasy? I hope never to confront such a difficult decision again. I told him I needed a month's break from his secrets. I would not see him, but we exchanged friendly texts while we were both free to date others. The amicable month passed. Now we entered the park, wondering what would happen next.

Act I: The Picnic Table

Tall Norfolk pines allowed afternoon sunlight to slice between them; an almost liquid yellow filled the air with Hawaiian warmth even at a couple thousand feet. If these stately tall trees were guardians, they would say to the sunlight, "Okay, come in and have your fun, but no wild stuff. We maintain dignified standards here." A few family groups sat on blankets; young people entered and exited the hiking trails into deep forest.

As I knew he would, Evan scouted out the most hidden, covered, picnic area, where we sat at a long green wooden table, classic park department style. Both a little shy after our separation, we sat a foot apart. But as we chatted, the inches slowly disappeared, much to my delight. Did I mention that his touch on my arm sent electricity flying up, around my back and down to the opposite hand? Evan, with his broad rugged face, was stocky and muscular, and edged closer to me. After furtive glances to make sure we were unobserved, we kissed. The voltage now on a vertical trajectory, burst into my brain and down to my nether regions. My breath quickened.

When I spied walkers approaching at a distance, we separated, but he drew my legs across his lap. I noticed a mosquito bite or two. Hawaiian mosquitos are polite: gentle and silent, and they cause a minor itch that soon passes. I decided to ignore them in favor of my comfort with Evan: surrounded by trees as tall and straight as the pillars of a Greek temple, high rectangles of sun whose warmth gently touched my skin, the sweet smell of pine and the entrancing medleys of more songbirds than I ever remembered hearing in one place.

Act II: Chicken Families

In this contented intimacy, I looked around and saw families of wild chickens, common to all the Hawaiian Islands, their little chicks foraging on the forest floor while trying to keep up with their moms. It was late spring, the same season I had watched the baby chicks grow in our chicken coop at home during all of my childhood years. Our cute little chicks grew up and we eventually ate them, but each spring, I coveted the new babies with no thought for the future.

These wild babes stuck close to their mom while the cock

strolled at a distance, seeming to keep watch.

The chickens were tamed to the visitors who strolled by and casually observed them. The mother chicken scratched at the pine needle turf with hard kicks, left, right, left; then she would peck at the bugs she uncovered. Tiny balls of fluff scurried to keep up, trying to stay at her head, I noticed. When one strayed to the rear, it received a swift, powerful kick and quickly ran back to its mom's head, haphazardly pecking at the earth, just as she did. Mom was a one-chicken pre-school and a tough-love teacher like all good mothers.

When I watched a family group with older chicks, I saw that these kids were able to consistently kick and uncover bugs on their own with strong sure legs, as if they were in chicken elementary school. How quickly they had learned. And yet these youngsters, perhaps a quarter the size of an adult, could have fit in my hand.

I'd never seen such a large flock of wild chickens. There were perhaps thirty or more. They calmly fed off the mountain, seemingly at the top of the Hawaiian food chain, no one wanting to eat them.

Act III: Rain

Strong wind scattered leaves from the tall mountain apple trees, the bushy red guava trees and needles from the ironwoods. In Hawaii, volcanic upheavals thrust the land into sharp vertical heights not far from the ocean. Our park was only about 100 feet wide, located at the start of a narrow trail on a ridge line. From our perch, we watched dark clouds swirl below and above us. A hard rain played timpani with loud "pings" on the metal roof above our table. We huddled closer, glad for the excuse, cozy in our shelter while we watched the slanting gray rains rush to earth and felt their dampness on our arms and legs. As if the sudden rushing water had entered stage right, it declared, "I am Great Nature who can whoosh in and out, stunning and drenching you in a moment." The rains had sent the walkers dashing to their cars for shelter and gave us more privacy, which we used for extra smooches.

With my head on Evan's wide shoulder, I watched the hard rain and remembered that our ridgeline at the peak of the Pali (as these mountains are called) was known as the birthplace of the trade winds, a cool respite from tropical heat. High cool air from the Pacific swept in and hit the mountain tops, then made an abrupt downward u-turn. The "gusty trades" rattled windows and doors as they swooped down Manoa valley at land level, providing natural air conditioning. I lived in this valley for twelve years; each bedroom door was wedged tight with socks to stop the rattles all night long, the socks drooped on the outside of each door frame of our three bedrooms like relaxed phallic totems.

Act IV: Stealth Swarm

When the rains eased, we wandered down a trail to a park

restroom, not holding hands, which seemed too intimate for our current situation. When I emerged from the women's room, Evan paced, concerned. "I found these little ants on me," he said, pointing to his feet, clad in open flip-flop sandals. "I think you should check yourself." After living in Hawaii for twenty years, I had seen plenty of tiny rust-colored ants, about one-eighth of an inch long, but on Evan's stubby feet were what looked like specks of black dirt. Even with my best glasses on, I could discern no segmented body or waving antennae.

"How could those be ants?" But I had long ago ceded to Evan's superior eyesight and we quickly ascertained that everywhere my peach-colored clothes had made contact with the park picnic table was covered with tiny black moving dots. "Yuck," I cried, flailing my arms as I brushed at my chest and waist. "I'm infected." What if they were tiny ticks, a micro land crab or, worse, lice? I needed a complete brush-down and Evan was happy to oblige. A horse's curry brush would have been ideal, but Evan made do with his hands, vigorously swishing my back side while I stomped and swiped my hands across my legs and feet. Dark flecks flew.

A viewer might think we were engaged in a tribal mating dance, and she wouldn't have been far from wrong. If I could name these ants, they would be called a Stealth Swarm. But, happily, this new breed provided the perfect excuse for the all-body pat-down we both craved. In turn, I swatted at Evan's back, having spotted a multitude of the miniature ants on his beige cotton shirt (freshly ironed with crisp creases along the sleeves that he pressed himself, a major turn on and another reason to question my celibacy). Unfortunately, his shorts were black so I had no excuse to swat them. Friendly butt slaps were too familiar, but I eyed his rear, a superior specimen, hoping to see little moving particles. No luck.

Act V: The Narrow Ridge

Evan had checked my neck and hair for the marauding insects and found nothing. At last, with a final peek down the inside back of my tank top, he declared me free. But I still twitched with phantom creepy crawlies and couldn't sit still. "Let's head up that ridge trail," I said pointing. Evan didn't hike. In fact, he rarely walked. He was a man's man: he loved his car, insisting on driving me a block from my condo to get coffee or go to the beach. I was surprised when he acquiesced, but shouldn't have been; the trail led into the quiet, secluded forest.

I could never resist a mountain trail, eager to see what would appear around the next bend. Evan's strategy was to ask the few other hikers what was ahead. From an overweight middle-aged couple exiting the trail, we heard there might be a bench with a good view a few hundred yards in, but they hadn't gotten that far. Fifty feet up the trail, a solitary fifteen-year-old boy with braces said there was no such bench, but he pointed out a secret trail through the guava and ironwood trees that made a loop and came back to the main trail farther ahead. He took off at a trot on this trail; otherwise we wouldn't have been able to see this vague path.

Intrigued, I followed at a slow pace. Evan surprisingly willing, held branches back to make my way upward easier. After fifteen minutes or so we came to a clearing with remnants of a bonfire. Through the abundant foliage, it was a shock to see that we stood on a cliff edge that plunged more than a thousand feet. I clutched at Evan as we peered into the abrupt drop-off, Palolo valley. Slowly, we recognized landmarks. Near the ocean, Koko Head crater formed a perfect large green circle.

Saturated with the splendor, we drew back a few feet and predictably grew more interested in each other. At last we had the complete solitude that had probably made Evan willing to hike. Evan put his arm around me and I demurely turned toward him, unsure of how close I wanted to get, since my status as a secret in his life hadn't changed in the past month. But his touch did its usual magic. When he pulled my hair back and nuzzled my neck, I looked up at the mountain apples with joy. His embrace tightened and I turned my face to gently gnaw on his high cheekbones, familiar and warm, then slid my tongue down into his full mouth. The sun, the musty smell of the ironwoods, the crisp mountain air swirled into one unified sensation of pure thrill. We remained standing, no lolling on the ground subconsciously wary of strange new insect life.

All at once, from the dense trees surrounding us, out popped the fifteen-year-old with braces. Evan saw him first, and hastily dropped his arms to his sides, while I flailed, nearly losing my balance. "Oh, man, I'm so sorry," Evan said to the boy as he fluttered his hands towards him, as if unsure of the right gesture for the occasion.

"Uh, yeah, it's okay, whatever," the boy stammered.

And, belatedly, from me came, "I'm really sorry." It took me awhile to recover from the swoon Evan produced.

The flushing boy rushed past us and out of the clearing, apparently following the invisible track. The poor teenager was probably running up and down this steep trail to wear down frustrated sexual energy, and found us, the very fantasy he was in all likelihood trying to defuse. Our passion lay shattered on the ground, no doubt food for the bizarre new insect varieties Mother Nature was creating.

"Well..." Evan and I spoke at the same time.

I was abashed; the teenager had showed us his special trail and we had violated it.

We decided to head back, and just in time, as when we came to the end of the trail, our old friend, Hard Rain, entered stage right from the Manoa Valley side. We scurried to the car but not before we were drenched.

229

Act VI: Hunting Dogs

In the steaming car, we relaxed, safe from rain, ants and each other in the populated parking lot. Like us, other hikers and walkers had rushed to their cars. By late afternoon, the picnic areas were deserted.

As tropical rains tend to do, however, they passed within twenty minutes or so and the sun re-emerged. While I patted my clothes and Evan's shirt to see if they had dried yet, we chatted like old friends.

A few parking slots below us, a pick-up truck arrived. A young woman released a passel of dogs that immediately ran helter-skelter all around the park. Luckily, there were no picnickers with young children. The woman eventually called to the dogs and walked with them. All six were running free, unleashed, toward the untended far end of the park where few people went. Still, six dogs created a hunting pack.

I glanced around and saw that small groups of the pecking chickens had wandered to the broad grass and pine needle areas near the picnic tables in front of us. Zeus had thrown a lightning bolt into the peaceful park: a pack of six dogs and a large flock of tame feeding fowl. I instantly foresaw an imminent chicken massacre.

I had long ago learned that consequences that seemed obvious to me were typically invisible to others. An ex-boyfriend had described this characteristic as my pessimism; a conclusion that was grossly unfair in my estimation. As I had explained to him for many years, I could simply see likelihoods. Evan lounged in the driver's seat, oblivious. When I explained the turn of events about to happen, he shrugged.

"The chickens will see the dogs and fly away," he said simply.

"But, they're tame. They're not on the lookout. They won't see the dogs in time."

What seemed clear as a blinking neon light to me did not faze Evan, the other park-goers, the dog-owner or the chickens. I could have relaxed and let nature take its course. It would be no worse than what fast food restaurants caused to happen every day when they bought thousands of chicken carcasses to create McNuggets. It would be no worse than what my dad did to feed our family when I was young.

As I watched the scene unfold, I realized I could help these particular chickens. From the corner of my eye, I saw the leader of the pack, the largest dog, making a beeline toward our car where more chickens had gathered to form a group of about thirty little souls. I jumped out of the car and began to clap my hands and yell at the chickens. "Go! Go! Scat! Get out of here!"

The dignified fowl calmly glanced my direction as if to say, "What's wrong with that strange human? We get all types in this park."

I chased the chickens toward the rim of the steep ridge, heavy with bushes and small trees, where they could find cover. They walked a few steps, then went back to feeding; it was like trying to herd molasses.

The dogs drew nearer.

"GET! GO! Scram!" I clapped louder and stomped my feet. I didn't care what Evan thought of me. The flock reluctantly moved a few feet away. It was only when the dogs burst upon them that they finally took notice, running for cover and flying toward the low trees. Those that could fly made it to safety by the width of a feather, but I had forgotten about the babies who couldn't fly. Low to the ground, they ran and scrambled. Had they all made it? No, one hadn't. The lead dog chased it and grabbed it in his mouth. My heart thudded deep in my chest.

Belatedly, the dog-owner ran into the fray and forced the large dog to drop the chick. Miraculously, it continued to run. The woman yelled at me, "Grab the white dog. He's the one who'll go after the chick."

The white dog was a pit bull. I stared at the young woman as if she were nuts, which I had already decided she was, to illegally run a pack of dogs in a park where human infants had earlier been resting on picnic blankets. No way would I grasp a hunter, inflamed with the chase, whose jaw could easily break my arm. In the meantime, a rust-colored dog seized the chick in its mouth. Once again, my heart fell. Zeus would, it seemed,

232

have his way. But the woman pried open the dog's jaws and the chick popped out once again like an indestructible toy.

This time she snatched it, and stretching far over the top of her dogs, she handed the chick to me. I cradled the soggy lump whose bright eyes spied me and protested with loud peeps. Good, he was alive. I checked my hands to see if the chick had bled on me; no blood. I began to believe in immortality.

"We saved a life today," the woman crowed.

No thanks to your raging pack of canines, I thought as I gave her stink eye and stalked away. It's always hard to know how much to vent when someone deserves it, but I had learned the hard way that there's no need to rouse a looney to higher heights of craziness.

I cradled the youngster, apparently one of the elementary-aged chicks who knew how to kick and feed on his own already. As I walked it toward the rim, searching for the rest of the flock, I caught a waft of chicken smell and was flooded with memories of my childhood chicken coop. Thinking only of myself, I lowered my nose to the chick and inhaled deeply. How many satisfying childhood olfactory memories have we lost that we don't realize?

I looked to see the flock safely roosting in low trees and high bushes. Unfortunately, I did not realize that my nose was so close to my mouth, and to the chick no doubt, I was a large predator with jaws of death. Chirping loudly, its mom answered from a nearby tree, the chick burst from my hands and fluttered on a downhill trajectory toward the ground, stumbling when it landed and rushing over toward Mom.

My hands held two small drops of the babe's blood, which had apparently oozed from a small wound; not bad for having inhabited two dog mouths.

<u>Act VII: Clean Up</u>

Evan had emerged from his car and watched my antics with raised eyebrows and an unbelieving expression. *Odd*, I thought. *He's a retired EMT ambulance driver with thirty-seven years aiding others.*

"You saved the chick," he said, perhaps with admiration.

"I hope so," I said. We both looked at my hands that I held in front of me, away from my body. Belatedly, I hoped they were not covered with chicken lice or poop. Evan noticed the two drops of chicken blood and scrambled for his emergency kit. After scrubbing with hand cleanser and sanitary wipes, I handed the debris to Evan who carried it to a trash can. I took a deep breath and gazed around the park. It was then that I became aware of my legs throbbing from so many mosquito bites. I saw large swollen red patches where the female bites clustered, nearly one on top of the other. I sighed. Today I had rescued a chick and donated dinner to a horde of starving insects. Real martyr qualifications.

The dog owner departed and peace returned the park to its

seemingly normal placidity. It was no longer a place where a glut of nature's perpetual blood-boiling scenarios reigned; where humans played at rash, juicy seduction; where sudden slicing rains sent creatures scurrying; where ants stormed living bodies to stake their claim; where flocks of fowl ate smaller creatures, and, in turn, fertilized the soil; where higher predators preyed on birds; where lifeblood fed a new generation of mosquitos.

In the pastoral woodlands, nature's furious cycles held sway: the rhythms of birth, infancy, growing, gaining mastery, coupling, creating, and dying. Entering that park we unknowingly became Epic Evan and Cathartic Cate, one with the environment's timeless and volcanic stage set, its eternal lust for itself in a relentless archetypal world, our parts as inevitable as all the other creatures.

We had arrived in the park wondering what would happen next. Now I knew. Evan's weird secret life with me as the mystery woman was too loaded for me. Nature's bloodlust dramas and I could now part ways, for Mother Nature with her powerful prototypes reminded me that the stakes were high and not to mess with her if I was going to be uncertain or dwell in trifles. I ducked out of the line of fire. Adios, Evan.

Chapter 39
Ultimate Alice

"I don't have good memories. I don't have bad memories. I just have memories." Ninety-five-year-old Alice fixed me with a defiant stare over my suggestion that her husband's many years as a musician in the philharmonic orchestra must have left her lovely reminiscences to look back upon.

I had been forewarned about Alice's state of mind. When I first arrived, I had remarked on the beautiful day, prompting her to say, "It's not beautiful. It's not ugly. It's just a day. Every day I sit in this chair. The days come and go and they are not getting better."

Admittedly, Alice's reality made perfect sense for someone in her tenth decade. As a hospice volunteer, I imagined my mission was to bring light and joy to the suffering. But, not only did Alice reject my rosy visions, they offended her.

After several Pollyanna parries, I finally looked in the

mirror hanging behind Alice's head on her kitchen wall. When I spotted a hopeful smile on my face, I wiped it off. My positivity track record in my own life stank; my efforts toward a prestigious job and an enviable marriage had left me with part-time low-wage work and philandering boyfriends whose escapades I had successfully ignored for many years.

Alice's sharp glances inspired me to try to see reality instead of Camelot. I refocused on the back of Alice's head, also visible in the mirror; thin gray strands of hair allowed her skull to shine with a pink gleam. Her spiky, stick-like shoulders were so insubstantial, her dress kept sliding off of them. She had lost weight in the last three months since I had begun to visit her, and my heart ached to see her so tender and vulnerable.

Alice hunched in her kitchen chair, her back bone curved with the weight of her many years. With her pixie haircut, pointed chin and one good eye, she could have starred in the Harry Potter books and movies as a house elf; her cunning temperament fit the part, too.

From past experiences, I knew that once Alice slipped into contrarian mode, she would stay entrenched for an hour or more. Since she lacked short-term memory, we had a weekly enactment of the Groundhog Day movie; with each visit, I had to get to know her all over again. Unfortunately, she did not remember that she did not remember. If I said I'd been visiting her for three months, her eyebrows arched in suspicion. "I've never seen you before." I could tell she wondered what kind of scheme I was trying to pull off. But if I told her she had lost her short-term memory, even if she believed me, ten minutes later, she would forget I had told her.

When I first arrived, she would often interrogate me. "Why are you sitting in my kitchen/bedroom/living room? Where did you come from? Are you someone off the street? What are you doing here? Why would a complete stranger want to visit me?" She made a good point. One would imagine I could use the answers that had worked best in previous weeks, hoping to shorten the interrogation period. But once she became an impish diva, she always used her full hour to lambaste me.

Mostly unsuccessful, my strategies for coping with abrasive personalities were threefold:

1. Spread illusions of sweetness and light; in other words, pretend the problem does not exist. Fortunately, Alice did not permit myopic pleasantries.

2. Cave into submissive hopelessness and let the aggressor dominate while hoping to soon flee. When this old habit took over (the way to survive two older sisters), Alice usually ignored me. One time, she tried to jolly me out of my moody silence; my sisters had never bothered, so Alice's effort provided a healing balm to me. "Look at the sunlight on the tree leaves," she said. With eyes lifted to this simple joy, we talked about the wind and the changing, flickering light.

Surrendering as I had done to passivity, I felt like a cowardly Hospice volunteer. But I rationalized that Alice liked to take over in her chatty way, thus I justified making her do all the work of socializing, which would have been a real chore for my introverted personality. "The light isn't good and it isn't bad. It just is," Alice reminded me.

"You're right. It just wonderfully *is,*" I replied, adding, "I love how your mind works."

3. Be brave and strong. Gather all my chutzpah to the fore, allowing me to be just as brazen as her. With great valor, I would pump up my confrontational energies and remember my testosterone supplement, a tiny time-release pellet shoved under my skin bi-annually. In times of need, I imagined this Raging Bull stream of courage flowing into every cell and I would silently chant, "I can do this. I can do this." I needed all my assertiveness training techniques to amp me up to use flattery and stand-up comedy to dispel Alice's suspicions of me.

The best way to soften Alice up was to compliment her. Yes, I know: It's cheap. Intelligent and eloquent, Alice made it easy because she had lived an enviable and exotic life filled with adventure. Her long-term memory made up for whatever happened ten minutes ago. I didn't have to lie to flatter Alice, I just had to bring up topics that cast her into old memories: tap dancing, being onstage as a mime in Europe, fleeing from

Joseph McCarthy, and later in exile, Radio Free Prague. With each memory elicited, I remembered to shamelessly blast out a true-as-possible compliment, such as "What an amazing life you've had." I have since noticed this is a good skill to use on everyone I meet.

Another way to halt her introductory berating session was to tell jokes. My lousy dates were usually enough to start her giggling. I had learned through dogged experience that laughter inspired trust. Unfortunately, a very narcissistic woman I knew could keep folks in an uproarious state. Naturally, everyone trusted her, a grossly displaced group delusion; that's how I learned this quirk of human nature. Using it with Alice created a little guilt, but my ends were benign, thus I justified the means (as I am sure all criminals must do). Regardless, it was fun. After several references to my dismal love life, Alice softened up. When I threw in as many praises as my conscience could bear, her eyebrows lowered and she would sweetly say, "It can take awhile to feel okay with a person, can't it?"

I would smile and agree, "You're very right, as usual."

Inspired by some cue invisible to me, after an hour, Alice turned off the interrogation lamp and relaxed. While we laughed and chatted like schoolgirls, she was an angel. I could tell that she thrived on our give and take. But I couldn't help but think that I would have to repeat the first hour's rite of passage next week. Will I run Alice's gauntlet with my usual whitewashing attempts to make everything beautiful? Or will I descend into a passive lump and let Alice lead the way? Or will I gather my puny efforts as a brown-noser and stand-up comic? Probably some messy combination of all three, as usual.

Lately, toward the end of Alice's cross-examination hour, I've become tempted to say, "Look, whether you're ninety-five years old or not, I don't put up with rude behavior. Be nice or I go." As a stop-gap measure, this has worked with various boyfriends, but they couldn't sustain kindness for very long. I suspect that Alice, lacking short-term memory, would be the same. Perhaps that was the problem with the boyfriends, too. Meanwhile, for the sake of maintaining the angelic hospice image, I have focused on my main three standbys with Alice.

When our time was up, I asked her like always, "Would you like me to visit next week?"

"Oh, of course. I'd love that," extroverted Alice said, her good eye twinkling at the prospect. As I stood to leave, I pulled the neck of her dress up over her emaciated shoulder. Tough and fragile all at once, Alice inspired me to be the same; face reality with zest and with sweetness. As I left, we squeezed hands and kissed good-bye with affection.

I sighed, knowing next week would be a good visit at least for half the time.

Chapter 40
A Quiet and Sweet Landing

I am a flashing green eye. Humans worship me with offerings of large amounts of jade-colored paper for what they call an emerald, their name for me. I sit on a sacred golden hoop, dazzling all who come near my usual perch on an ear. My sister sits on the other ear; we are always together, either in the jewelry box or on opposite sides of a head. For many years, I have tried to hide my powers of x-ray vision from my sister. My inner striations hold a special frequency that she does not have, and I don't want her to feel badly. But it's hard to dumb down for her, hour after hour, day after day. I want to share what I see underneath people's clothes, beneath their skin, inside their bones and what I can hear in their minds.

After all these years together, I have become a middle-aged earring and I need to bust out, to live my full potential. One day, I decide to escape from my sister. The living room couch in our house is where the most interesting things happen. And since I don't have a stomach, the kitchen pales in importance. When my earring-holder (a human) sits on the sofa to trim her toenails, I slowly disengage the clasp that holds me to her; I lightly drop onto soft beige leather, a quiet and sweet landing. To hide, I roll into a nearby crevice and cuddle in a little bend in the thin hide. My single sparkling eye looks up. I can see through my human's clothes into her underwear. That thong looks extremely uncomfortable and not too hygienic. But she expects her boyfriend later today. What humans will do for mating rituals.

Her toes tidy by now, I perk up when my human lies on the couch to meditate. She's good at clearing the day's clutter from her mind. I could care less about the driver who cut her off in traffic or the building violations at the construction site across the street. But when she gets through the junk and climbs into her third eye, we are in for a blissful ride. I piggyback as she floats on a lavender and navy aurora borealis of the mind. And I feel her deepest longing: to be in love with the divine. We journey with empty freedom in union with the sacred, a quiet and sweet landing.

All too soon, the door clicks open and my human leaps up to greet her son and his girlfriend. I don't know why she feels a little guilty about the deep meditation we have so abruptly abandoned. Perhaps she wants her son to think she is busy so he won't worry about her. She hugs the young couple with genuine affection, says, "Love you," then she whisks away on her date.

At times, the two twenty-five-year-olds passionately fight on the couch, words and tears flying like ninja blades. But today they sink into the soft cushions to compare apps on their phones, and debate the virtues of this one and that. It's amazing how hairy the male butt is compared to the female. The young woman sits close to me and I can clearly see that her spine is already curved, humping forward where she has, for years, hunched her shoulders down to disguise her full six foot height. "Oh dear, dear girl," I say with green tears in my eyes, "keep your shoulders back and raise your sternum high to the world." I pour my bright vibrations into her bones, hoping they hear me.

Perhaps they do, for her hand suddenly knocks me over. "Hey, what's this?" she calls. She fumbles with me and lifts me high in the air, like I'm on a rollercoaster, rising to the apex. "Isn't this your mom's earring?" she asks the human's wide-jawed son with the curly hair. His olive eyes meet mine, and I remember all the years of his youth when I poured my green energies into his as he grew, cell by cell. The hue of his eyes reflects my many years of devotion to him.

"Oh yeah, that's Mom's. It must have fallen off her ear. I'll put it in her jewelry case."

I sigh as my green-eyed boy carries me away. My sibling is out enjoying the human's date. But, I know, when she returns, I'll find the right moment to share my adventures with her. I think she'll understand that we are different and I must honor my abilities at long last. And now that I've seen how easy it is to travel, I'll do it more often; she might want to join me sometimes. The human's son gently sets me in the spot where my sister and I usually nest, a quiet and sweet landing.

About the Author

Cate Burns has lectured and taught internationally at universities in Prague, The Czech Republic, New York City, Los Angeles and other cities. She holds a BA degree from the University of Washington in Asian Studies, a second BA degree from the University of Nevada Las Vegas in Fine Arts, an MFA from the University of California Irvine in Fine Arts, and a PhD from the Union Graduate School in Art History and Women's Studies. She is a recipient of an Elizabeth Morse Genius Foundation Award from the National Association of Women Artists in New York City, The Twentieth Century Award for Achievement, the International Woman of the Year Award from the International Biographical Centre, London. She won first place for her non-fiction short story, The Girdle, from the national competition, the Lorin Tarr Gill Writing Contest. Her book manuscript, Libido Tsunami, won an award as an unpublished manuscript in the Pacific Rim Book Festival in 2016.

If you enjoyed *Libido Tsunami,* consider these other fine books from
Savant Books and Publications:

Essay, Essay, Essay by Yasuo Kobachi
Aloha from Coffee Island by Walter Miyanari
Footprints, Smiles and Little White Lies by Daniel S. Janik
The Illustrated Middle Earth by Daniel S. Janik
Last and Final Harvest by Daniel S. Janik
A Whale's Tale by Daniel S. Janik
Tropic of California by R. Page Kaufman
Tropic of California (the companion music CD) by R. Page Kaufman
The Village Curtain by Tony Tame
Dare to Love in Oz by William Maltese
The Interzone by Tatsuyuki Kobayashi
Today I Am a Man by Larry Rodness
The Bahrain Conspiracy by Bentley Gates
Called Home by Gloria Schumann
Kanaka Blues by Mike Farris
First Breath edited by Z. M. Oliver
Poor Rich by Jean Blasiar
Ammon's Horn by Guerrino Amati
The Jumper Chronicles by W. C. Peever
William Maltese's Flicker by William Maltese
My Unborn Child by Orest Stocco
Last Song of the Whales by Four Arrows
Perilous Panacea by Ronald Klueh
Falling but Fulfilled by Zachary M. Oliver
Mythical Voyage by Robin Ymer
Hello, Norma Jean by Sue Dolleris
Richer by Jean Blasiar
Manifest Intent by Mike Farris
Charlie No Face by David B. Seaburn
Number One Bestseller by Brian Morley
My Two Wives and Three Husbands by S. Stanley Gordon
In Dire Straits by Jim Currie
Wretched Land by Mila Komarnisky
Chan Kim by Ilan Herman
Who's Killing All the Lawyers? by A. G. Hayes
Ammon's Horn by G. Amati
Wavelengths edited by Zachary M. Oliver
Almost Paradise by Laurie Hanan
Communion by Jean Blasiar and Jonathan Marcantoni
The Oil Man by Leon Puissegur
Random Views of Asia from the Mid-Pacific by William E. Sharp

248

The Isla Vista Crucible by Reilly Ridgell
Blood Money by Scott Mastro
In the Himalayan Nights by Anoop Chandola
On My Behalf by Helen Doan
Traveler's Rest by Jonathan Marcantoni
Keys in the River by Tendai Mwanaka
Chimney Bluffs by David B. Seaburn
The Loons by Sue Dolleris
Light Surfer by David Allan Williams
The Judas List by A. G. Hayes
Path of the Templar - Book 2 of The Jumper Chronicles by W. C. Peever
The Desperate Cycle by Tony Tame
Shutterbug by Buz Sawyer
Blessed are the Peacekeepers by Tom Donnelly/Mike Munger
Purple Haze by George B. Hudson
The Turtle Dances by Daniel S. Janik
The Lazarus Conspiracies by Richard Rose
Imminent Danger by A. G. Hayes
Lullaby Moon by Malia Elliott of Leon & Malia
Volutions edited by Suzanne Langford
In the Eyes of the Son by Hans Brinckmann
The Hanging of Dr. Hanson by Bentley Gates
Written in the Stars - An Anthology edited by Sabrina Favors
Elaine of Corbenic by Tima Z. Newman
Ballerina Birdies by Marina Yamamoto
More, More Time by David Seaburn
Crazy Like Me by Erin Lee
Cleopatra Unconquered by Helen R. Davis
Valedictory by Daniel Scott
The Chemical Factor by A. G. Hayes
Quantum Death by A. G. Hayes
Running against the Pack edited by Helen R. Davis
Big Heaven by Charlotte Hebert
Captain Riddle's Treasure by GV Rama Rao
All Things Await by Seth Clabough

Coming Works
The Adventures of Purple Head, Buddha Monkey and Sticky Feet by Erik Bracht
Cereus by Z. Roux
In the Shadows of My Mind by Andrew Massie
Finding Kate by A. G. Hayes

http://www.savantbooksandpublications.com